"Kenan, why do we have to be here so early?"

Kel complained as he shuffled on the basketball court. "It's still my sleepy time."

"Now it's your practice time. We have a week to get good enough to beat the McThunk brothers." Kenan bounced the basketball on the ground hard a couple of times to build up his confidence.

"It's not too late to leave town," Kel offered.

"Man, we can't leave town," Kenan stated authoritatively. "I mean, this is where our parents live. If we leave, who's gonna cook for us?"

"Good point," Kel conceded reluctantly.

"Now look, we have a whole week. We gotta try. I don't want to go around wearing a shirt that says 'loser' on it."

Kenan tossed the ball over to Kel, who plucked it from the air with ease. "All right, let's just shoot around a little to warm up first."

Kenan & Kel™ books:

Aw, Here It Goes!
Family and Food and Orange Soda
ALIENs
Summer Vacation
Kel Got Game

Look for these other Nickelodeon® books:

Good Burger™
Good Burger™ 2 Go
All That™: Fresh Out the Box

Available from POCKET Books

Steve Holland

AN ARCHWAY PAPERBACK
Published by POCKET BOOKS
New York London Toronto Sydney Tokyo Singapore

AN ARCHWAY PAPERBACK *Original*

An Archway Paperback published by
POCKET BOOKS, a division of Simon & Schuster Inc.
1230 Avenue of the Americas, New York, NY 10020

ISBN: 0-671-03576-2

First Archway Paperback printing July 1999

10 9 8 7 6 5 4 3 2

Front cover illustration by BLT Studio and Associates

Printed in the U.S.A.

For Mom and Dad

"**G**ood day, fellow book readers, and welcome to another fun-filled installment of Kenan and Kel. I am often referred to by those in the know as . . . Kenan!"

"And I'm often referred to as 'Hey you!'"

"Kel!"

"Fine! I'm also referred to as *Mr.* Hey You."

"Kel!"

"And Kel. I also go by Kel! There, are you happy?!"

"Pretty happy. Now for this book I thought we'd try something a little different."

"Oh, are we gonna perform the entire book naked?"

"Nah, Kel, of course not. Why would we do that?"

"Because, Kenan, it's a book. No one can tell if we're naked or not."

"Well, our picture is on the front of this book. And if we were naked, then I doubt that anybody would be reading this right now."

"Hey, Kenan, that makes me wonder."

"What does it make you wonder, Kel?"

1

"If no one was reading this right now, would we still be here?"

"I don't know, Kel. That is actually a very good question. Let's find out."

"But, Kenan. How do you find out? I mean, what if we disappear and never come back?"

"Hey you! Yeah, that's right, you reading the book right now. Don't look around, of course I'm talking to you. How many people are reading this right now?"

"Kenan, it's okay really. We don't—"

"Kel, don't be so rude. Can't you see I'm talking to that reader right now? Sorry for the interruption, reader. Now listen, we need you to do us a favor. Kind of an experiment. We need you to shut this book and then open it back up. That way we can see whether or not we're still here when no one is reading. So go ahead and close the book, now . . . I said, close the book. Look, buddy, we're not going on with the rest of the story until you cooperate. So if you ever want to get past this Open, you'd better close the book right now. I mean it . . . I'm not kidding . . . I'm—Oh, that's better."

"Oh good, you're back! Hey, thanks for your help! So Kel, what did you think? Were we still here when no one was reading?"

"It was hard to tell, it was so dark in here and you know that I'm afraid of the dark. Why do you have to play games with my emotions like that?"

"Well you know, Kel, if you like games, then we have quite the fun-filled book in store for you today."

"Really. I get to play games?"

"That's right."

"What games do I get to play?"

"If you want to find that out, then read on. Now come along, Scary!"

"Kenan? Do you really think I'm scary? Kenan? Do I get to play Duck, Duck, Goose? I like that game. Kenan? Where are you always running off to? Kenan? Awww, here it goes!"

CHAPTER ONE

The round orange ball flew up into the air, like a helium balloon or a brick that happened to be round and orange and, somehow, had the ability to fly. For one brief second, just as it reached the top of its climb, and just before it started to fall back down to the ground, the ball seemed to hang there, floating in midair against the backdrop of the brilliant blue Saturday sky.

Kel stared at it. His head tilted back, his mouth hung open, allowing the small gap between his two front teeth to be displayed fully in the afternoon sun as a small line of drool quietly made its escape from the corner of his lips. A bright blue fisherman's hat was pulled snugly down over his brow. He squinted, narrowing his eyes up into tiny slits on either side of his nose as he stared up, hypnotized by the orangy roundness of the ball.

The blank, emotionless expression that sat on Kel's face may have looked to the world like his brain had finally decided "What's the use?" and suddenly quit working. In actuality though, his blank stare hid a rush of mental activity. A flood of thoughts busily rushed around the inside of Kel's brain, colliding with each other like a deranged mob at a rock concert. The thoughts went a little something like this: *Whoa! Check out that ball flying through the air. Hey, that's what a flying saucer would look like . . . if flying saucers were orange . . . and round . . . and looked like basketballs. Maybe if the aliens were from a planet called Basketballius, then they would build spaceships that looked like that. That would be cool. Hey! Maybe basketballs are actually spaceships from other planets, and we just think that they're here for us to play games with. Wait a minute! Does that mean that aliens on other planets use our spaceships to play basketball with? No, that would be silly. The space shuttle would never bounce well enough to play basketball with.* And then, for no apparent reason, he also thought, *I wonder if cows make good pets?*

He was so lost in thought, he didn't seem to notice two vitally important facts. One: the basketball that had been thrown up into the air was now rapidly falling down out of the air and straight towards him. And two: someone was calling his name.

"Kel!" Kenan called from underneath the nylon mesh of the basketball net from where he had thrown the ball. "Kel!" he yelled again loudly, drumming his foot impatiently on the concrete of the playground's basketball court.

The playground wasn't very big. It was just large enough to accommodate the full-sized basketball court and still have a little room left over for swings and slides and monkey bars and other sorts of bars that had nothing whatsoever to do with monkeys. It was nestled in a green, tree-lined field not far from the nice residential street where Kenan Rockmore lived with his parents and sister.

"Kel, the ball!" Kenan tried to warn his best friend. But it was no use. Kel was too lost in thought to notice Kenan's warnings. What Kel did manage to notice, a half a second later, was the rubber orange basketball bouncing off his head with a loud springy thump.

The basketball rocketed back up into the air, came down again, and bounced its way off to the other side of the court.

A new, dazed look managed to replace the blank expression that Kel Kimble so often wore on his face. He rubbed his head, gingerly feeling the tender lump that was quickly growing on his scalp. All thoughts of cows and pets and basketball planets quickly vanished from his head and were replaced with the much simpler thought: *Ow!*

"That really hurt, Kenan!" Kel complained to his best friend, who was busy retrieving the ball as it quickly rolled away.

"Then maybe you should have caught the ball, bouncy," Kenan yelled back. "That way it wouldn't have knocked you in your head."

"Oh, yeah." Kel nodded.

"Hey, nice catch!" a low voice taunted from the sidelines.

Kenan glanced up as he snatched the ball from off of the ground. A tall, beefy-looking kid stood on the side of the court. His deep-set eyes seemed almost to be trying to hide behind his face and his thin lips were pulled back in a jeering sort of grin.

"You're really good," the kid ridiculed from the sidelines, twisting his mouth up into an ugly sneer.

"Hey, thanks," Kel smiled genuinely, bobbing his head up and down happily at the compliment. "That's real nice of you." Kel had never quite grasped the concept of sarcasm. In fact, Kel had never quite grasped a lot of concepts, like addition and subtraction and the fact that fungus was not a food.

Kenan quickly walked up, cradling the ball in his arms. "Forget them, Kel. Come on, let's play."

"Yeah, forget about us," suggested a shorter, stockier kid, who took a spot on the sidelines next to his friend. His smile spread across his giant, pumpkin-sized head like a jagged, smiling scar. "We're just gonna sit here and watch you guys for pointers . . . on how to be awful!" Pumpkin Head laughed out loud at his joke in short, sharp, machine-gun bursts of "Ha! Ha ha ha ha ha!" His friend joined in, adding his own snorting pig laugh to the mix.

Kel arched his head towards Kenan and said in a conspiratorial half whisper, "You know what, Kenan? I'm starting to think that when he said how good I was earlier, he didn't really mean it."

Kenan cocked his boyishly round face to the side, curiously. He didn't cock his head curiously because he was surprised that Kel was just catching on. No, Kenan had been Kel's best friend since they were kids. He knew Kel better than anybody in the world and what had surprised him was that Kel had actually caught on as quickly as he had. It wasn't that Kel was dumb. On the contrary, Kel did well in school and had even managed to score pretty high levels on their school's IQ tests. It was just that looking at him or talking to him or just being in his general vicinity, you would never know it. Kel lived in a world all his own. And in his world, things seemed to work a little differently. In his world, he was apparently unaware that the two taunting thugs on the sidelines were the playground's most notorious basketball sharks, Billy and Brian McThunk. The McThunk brothers were notorious for two reasons. First, they were the best amateur basketball players on this side of Chicago. They never lost. And second, because they were really, really bad winners. There was nothing they loved more than taunting other basketball players, like Kenan and Kel, until the other players, like Kenan and Kel, got so fed up that they would decide to teach the McThunks a lesson by challenging them to a game of basketball. At which point the McThunks would humiliate them on the court in front of anybody who happened to be watching, making it virtually impossible for the other basketball players, like Kenan and Kel, to ever show their sad, basketball-losing faces on the playground ever again.

Luckily Kenan knew all about Billy and Brian's devious little schemes and he wasn't about to fall into their trap. Unluckily, Kel had other plans.

"Hey, if you guys think you're so good, why don't you play us. Huh? What do you think about that?" Kel strutted across the court, a confident expression on his face. He shot a couple of smug, "don't worry" looks back at Kenan, who was just beginning the process of freaking out. "That's right, not so tough now are you?" Kel jeered at the brothers.

Kenan's large, brown eyes bugged out wide like two pie-shaped saucers that had been shot out of two pie-shaped cannons. Even the short stubby dreadlocks that drooped off of his head seemed to bolt upright in a sudden, hairy expression of shock. "Kel!" he exclaimed loudly, once his tongue recovered from the surprise.

"Don't worry, Kenan, I'm taking care of it."

"No! Not taking care of it! Taking care of it is something you're *not* doing." Kenan busily tried to get his brain under control and form a coherent sentence.

Billy McThunk craned the weight of his melon-sized head over to stare at his brother. Brian McThunk's razor lips parted and hung like two really skinny lip armies facing each other across the yellow battlefield of his teeth. There was a moment of silence between them.

The moment of silence ended as both brothers broke into snorting, chortling laughter. This harsh, unpleasant sound was accompanied by a lot of punching back and forth. It was what they did instead of speaking to one another. Instead of saying, "Good morning," to one another, Billy and Brian would trade punches. Instead of saying, "Would you like some lunch, brother?" they would trade punches. And on birthdays, the traditional McThunk happy birthday greeting was a headbutt, followed by a couple of swift kicks.

A hand shot out, snatched Kel by the scruff of the neck and yanked him aside. "Kel, what are you doing?" Kenan demanded, his voice shaking slightly with a touch of panic.

"Oh, see," Kel began to explain. "I know exactly what I'm doing."

"I know what you're doing too," Kenan snapped back. "You're gonna get us destroyed out here. We can't beat those guys." Images of their soon-to-be-humiliating doom rushed through Kenan's head like snapshots from a really gruesome book. It didn't look pretty. His mind quickly shifted gears and began trying to find a good getaway plan.

"Okay, here's what we can do. I'll fake a sprained

liver and while I'm flopping around on the ground, moaning and groaning, you yell for someone to get an ambulance. Then, we can make our getaway." Kenan nodded his head as he finished. It wasn't the best of plans, but it would have to do.

"Kenan, we can't run away from these guys. They're just bullies. And my momma always told me that bullies are all talk, all you have to do is to stand up to them."

"All talk?!" Kenan hissed. "Have you been listening? These guys can barely talk at all. What they can do is play basketball, really, really well."

"We can beat them," Kel reassured his friend calmly. He placed an arm lightly around Kenan's shoulder like a coach preparing his star player for the big game. "See, we have to win. We're good and they're bad. We're nice and they're mean. We're . . . uh . . . milk and they're sheep with really bad athlete's foot. We're small frogs from the swamps of—"

"All right. I get it. Just please stop talking." Kenan grabbed his friend's hand between two fingers as if it were a dead skunk, and quickly plucked it from his shoulder.

Billy McThunk lugged his oversized noggin onto the court and settled it directly in front of Kenan's far more normal sized head. He breathed out in hot, smelly puffs and Kenan had to turn his head away.

"Not planning on chickening out are you, chicken?"

"Ohhh, had a little tuna there for lunch, did you?" Kenan asked as he fanned a hand rapidly in front of his nose, desperately trying to blow the foul smell away to someone else's nostrils.

Brian joined his brother, jabbing a beefy finger into Kenan's chest. "You're going down . . . punk!" he hissed as the two of them crowded in front of Kenan.

Kenan swallowed hard, trying not to show fear. Playground lore had it that the McThunks were like dogs: they could smell fear. And who was Kenan to argue with the wise kids who handed down playground wisdom from generation to generation, passing on such useful tidbits as "If you touch your tongue to a cold metal pole, it will stick," and "If you stick your tongue to the road, it will get run over," and of course, the ever useful, "If you stick your tongue to a skunk, it will taste really, really bad."

Kel butted in at Kenan's side and stared down the brothers McThunk. "Let's play!" he growled.

The brothers nodded in unison and with matching smiles on their lopsided heads, they turned and marched off, preparing to defend the basket.

"We're gonna get creamed," Kenan squealed, scrunching his features up until his face seemed almost a full two inches shorter than it was before.

"Don't worry, Kenan. I got it all figured out." Kel glanced slyly from side to side to make sure no one was close enough to hear his plan. It was clever. It was simple. It was brilliant. It was this: "See, all we have to do is get the ball and put it in the net more times than they do." His wide bright eyes met Kenan's own disbelieving gaze with a proud glint. "Eh? Eh?" he prompted, waiting for Kenan to give him his proper due.

"Whhhhhyyyyyyyy!" was all Kenan said before Kel grabbed the ball, rushed behind the line, and threw it in bounds. The game had begun.

Six and a half minutes later, it was all over. The small cloud that drifted lazily across the sun barely had time to reach the other side before Kenan and Kel had managed to lose the game by a staggering score of . . .

"Twenty to nothing! You lose! Losers!" Melon Head spat out loudly.

"Yeah," agreed his brother, "you guys are the worst . . . ever! My dog plays better than you two."

Kel looked up surprised. "Really, your dog can play basketball? That's amazing. That must be one incredible dog."

"No," Brian explained slowly. "See, my dog can't really play basketball, I just said that to illustrate how bad you two are. See?"

A smile lit up Kel's face and he bobbed his head up and down in understanding. "Oohhhhhh!"

Kenan's head hung low in shame, as if it were suddenly too heavy for his neck to hold up. He shook his round head back and forth sadly. "Man, we didn't even score once. It was like a nightmare. Except that in a nightmare at least they could have turned into big monsters and eaten us, so we wouldn't have to live with the humiliation. This is worse than a nightmare."

Kel shook his head as he approached Kenan. "You were right, Kenan, we can't beat those guys."

Kenan didn't lift his head up, but he shot a glance out from under his lowered eyelids. "Ya think?" he uttered with as much sarcasm as he possibly could.

Kel didn't seem to notice. "Well, yeah, I mean, they did just beat us. Weren't you paying attention?"

"Hey everybody!" Brian yelled from deep within his stocky, round belly. "Take a look at the losers!"

A crowd of playground kids had gathered around during the brief time that the game was going on and the McThunks were now busily showing off for them.

"Yeah, twenty to nothing! You know what, those guys could have not shown up and done just as well!" The brothers laughed loudly and obnoxiously.

Kenan gritted his teeth and set his jaw in firm determination.

Billy tilted his large head back and yelled over to Kenan and Kel, "Hey, boys, maybe you should try a different sport. I hear the loser-a-lympics are looking for a few good losers!"

"Yeah!" Brian chortled in agreement. "Or maybe you could take up water ballet!"

The gathered crowd began to laugh along with the McThunks, partially because they thought it was funny, but mostly because they were glad that it wasn't them being picked on by the two bad brothers.

Kenan's face began to twitch and then to tremble. His eye quivered like there was an earthquake going on in his brain. His lip shook like a starving man at first sight of food. His cheeks seemed to come alive as if under some strange cheek power all their own.

Kel eyed his friend curiously. "Hey, Kenan, are you okay, you look all twitchy."

"Someone needs to teach those guys a lesson," Kenan grumbled.

"Yeah, but who?"

Kenan's head began nodding up and down slowly, like he was agreeing with some unknown voice in his head. "Us, Kel."

"I don't know, Kenan, 'cuz we just lost really, really badly and now everyone is laughing at us. I'm not sure they learned their lesson."

Billy scampered over to them, not quite ready to let the taunting end. They had missed out on some of their early taunting time, and they weren't about to let another opportunity slip through their beefy little fingers.

"Hey, you guys need some directions to get home? We wouldn't want you to *lose* your way, since you seem so good at *losing* stuff."

Every muscle in Kenan's body tensed up. He tried to control himself. Tried to fight off the mistake that was about to come, but he just couldn't help it. He had been pushed to far.

"That does it, McThunks! You may have beat us today, but that was just luck."

Brian's wide smile grew a little bit wider. This was even better than he had expected. Kenan was actually going to have a meltdown right here in front of all these people. This was quickly becoming one of Brian's best days ever.

Billy spoke up first. "We don't need luck when we're playing chumps like you."

"Oh yeah? Oh yeah . . . well . . ." Kenan had passed the point of no return. He had dug his hole and now he had to jump in it. There was no turning back. "Well, then I hope you're up for a rematch. 'Cuz Kel and me will beat you anywhere, anytime, any . . . uh . . . where or time."

"Oh, this is just too good," Billy said. "But why should we play you again when we've already beaten you so badly?"

"That's a good question, Kenan," Kel whispered to his friend with a nod.

"Thank you, Kel." Kenan stalled for time as he tried to think of a good reason. "Because, whoever loses the next game has to walk around for a week wearing big shirts that say, 'I'm a loser'!" he finally blurted out, then winced as he heard exactly what it was he just said.

A look of concern suddenly spread across Kel's face. "Uh, Kenan, I don't think that's a very good idea. You know, 'cuz, they really are a lot better than us."

Brian McThunk's lips stretched wide in a huge, joyous grin. This was almost too good to be true. His brother would have also smiled as big if he weren't so busy trying to keep his huge head from toppling him over.

"Oh, you're on. One week from today, right back here."

Kenan swallowed hard and wondered why he couldn't have just walked away. Why he had to open his mouth and say something. Kel was actually wondering something a little more practical.

"Kenan, how are we gonna beat them?"

"Well." Kenan tried to sound confident, like he had a plan. It didn't work very well. "We have a week. We just have to practice until we're good enough to beat them."

"I have a better idea," Kel offered slowly and thoughtfully.

"Really? What is it?" Kenan asked, his desperation apparent.

"No, I'm just kidding. We're gonna lose after all."

Kenan's face fell. Kenan's stomach fell. Even Kenan's small intestine fell, coming to rest around the area his large intestine would have taken up if it also hadn't sagged with the sad sense of defeat. They were doomed.

CHAPTER TWO

The early morning sun cut through the fog of the cool Chicago dawn. Dewdrops gleamed in the new light as they clung to the green grass and the green leaves and the green painted square on the backboard of the basketball hoop for dear dew life.

Kenan and Kel rolled their bikes to a stop and leaned them against the damp trunk of a nearby tree. They stepped slowly onto the court. It was empty and silent.

"Kenan, why do we have to be here so early?" Kel complained as he shuffled onto the court. "It's still my sleepy time."

"Now it's your practice time. We have a week to get good enough to beat those guys." Kenan bounced the ball on the ground hard a couple of times to build up his confidence.

"It's not too late to leave town," Kel offered hopefully as he rubbed his hands together to try to stay warm in the cool morning air.

"Man, we can't leave town," Kenan stated authorita-

16

tively. "I mean, this is where our parents live. If we leave, who's gonna cook for us?"

"Good point," Kel conceded reluctantly.

"I know. Now look, we have a whole week. It's not like we're bad basketball players. We can do this, right?" he asked sheepishly.

Kel paused for a moment to consider it. "No," he answered finally.

Kenan threw his arms down in frustration. "Well, we gotta try. You don't want to go around wearing a shirt that says 'loser' on it, do you?"

"I don't know." Kel began chewing thoughtfully on his lower lip. "What color would the shirt be?"

With one eyebrow arched up towards his hair, Kenan raised one side of his lip and stared at his friend. "What difference would that make?"

"I don't know," Kel responded. "I mean, if it was, like, a nice blue shirt, that wouldn't be so bad."

Kenan fought hard to keep his voice calm. "It would still be a nice blue shirt that said 'loser' on it!" he said through clenched teeth.

"Yeah," Kel agreed cheerily. "Unless you were looking at it in a mirror; then it would say 'resol' on it."

"Uh-huh. Would you just take the ball." He tossed the ball over to Kel, who plucked it from the air with ease. "All right, let's just shoot around a little to warm up first."

Kel dribbled the ball on the cement in front of him, catching each upward bound with a flick of the palm that sent the ball careening back to the ground. He bent his legs, slightly hunching his body over the ball. Head tilted back, he eyed the target, the green square on the backboard that marked out the area the ball had to hit in order to rebound into the net. A couple of deep breaths and he was ready.

Grabbing the ball with both hands, he straightened his back, balanced the ball on his right palm, wrist back, guiding with the left hand, then finally popped the wrist and let the ball fly.

It spun through the air in a glorious arc. Kel watched intently as the ball sailed up into the sky, careened off the top edge of the backboard, rocketed straight up into the air, and finally came down, managing to avoid the vicinity of the net altogether.

Kenan snatched the ball from where it landed. He dribbled twice, then, fading back, launched himself into the air and shot. *Clang!* The sound of rubber bouncing off of metal rang loudly through the quiet morning air, as Kenan's shot bounced off of the rim and ricocheted back towards him.

Kel cut in front of him, snatching the ball off of one bounce. He dribbled low to the ground, driving up under the basket, then, as he passed underneath the hoop, he turned and shot. Off the backboard, the ball dropped down onto the lip of the rim. It ran a couple of quick, circular laps around the outside then slowed to halt, balancing precariously for a moment on the thin strip of metal from which the net hung, before slowly falling away from the net and back to the ground.

Kel grabbed his own rebound, took two small steps back from the basket, and lobbed up a light underhand shot that fell short of actually making it all the way to the net.

Kenan darted in from the outside and recovered the ball. He shot . . . and missed.

Kel's turn, the ball was up and down. Another miss. Kenan again: no good. Then Kel, almost but not quite.

Kenan: miss. Kel: miss. Kenan: another miss. Kel: not even close.

For close to half an hour, the horror raged on. Kenan and Kel, defying the odds, actually managed to miss every shot they put up. Even circus animals, statistically, would have accidentally made one eventually. But not Kenan and Kel. One miss after the next. Some close, some not so close. Some not even close to being not so close.

The sun rose way above the trees and began to warm the air as it beat down in earnest on the concrete court. The shrill whistling of the morning birds started to sound more like shrill laughing, as if the birds themselves were watching Kenan and Kel practice and mocking them.

Finally, Kenan grabbed the ball and stopped. He mopped at his dripping brow with the back of one arm and breathed in short and heavy breaths. He took a moment to regain his breath, which had apparently attempted to escape the embarrassment by going someplace else, then he turned to his friend and spoke. "Man!" Kenan figured that it pretty much summed up the situation.

Kel was also panting. He put his hands on his knees and leaned over them. "Yeah, how many baskets do you think we made there?"

"Well, Kel," Kenan spoke slowly, "I wasn't keeping too close a count. But it looked to me like . . . none!"

A small smile crept across Kel's narrow and sweaty face. "That many!" he exclaimed.

"This isn't working out at all!" Kenan laid the ball on the ground and sat on it. He ran his hands through his dreadlocks thoughtfully. "Okay, I got it!" he finally said. "We can't just keep shooting around like this.

That's not getting us anywhere. What we need to do is drill ourselves on each shot, one at a time."

Kel thought that that sounded like a fine plan, so he said, "That sounds like a fine plan," and waited for further instructions. Then, as he was waiting, he added, "Hey, Kenan, did you ever notice that a basketball looks kind of like a big orange baseball?" He nodded to himself at the accuracy of his observation.

Kenan squinted slightly at his friend. He had long since given up being surprised by most of what Kel blurted out. But from time to time, Kel could still manage to catch him off-guard. "You mean the way they're both . . . round?" Kenan asked skeptically.

Kel grinned broadly and bobbed his head up and down. "Yeah!" he exclaimed.

"Yes, Kel, that's quite a coincidence," Kenan humored his friend. "Now come on, let's get back to work." Kenan stood and shook his legs out a little as he held the ball between his two palms. "Let's practice our layups first."

Kel nodded as if he understood, and then, just to show that he didn't, he lay down on the ground. "Hey, Kenan. This concrete is kind of hot. How long do I have to lie here?"

Kenan glanced down at his friend, sprawled out across the cement. He knew he was going to regret asking the question that he was about to ask, but he decided to ask it anyway. "Kel . . . uh . . . what are you doing down there?"

"I'm practicing laying up. Just like you said. I think I'm pretty good at it, too." He shot a quick, confident thumbs-up in his friend's direction, then tried to concentrate on the business at hand.

Kenan gawked at his friend in stunned silence. He

did have to admit, though, Kel was pretty good at just lying there. If only it were a talent that was helpful in any way whatsoever, Kenan would have been incredibly proud of his friend's accomplishment. Unfortunately, since Kel's newfound ability would not help them in the least, now or ever, Kenan wasn't feeling very proud. What he was feeling was more like frustration. In fact, it was exactly like frustration, probably because it was frustration. "Would you get up!" he barked angrily. "I'm talking about the basketball shot!"

Kel flinched and quickly climbed to his feet, brushing the court dust off of his clothes as he stood. "Fine! You don't have to yell about it."

"We have to play the McThunks in six days," Kenan explained in a voice both loud and angry. "Do you have any idea what that means?"

"Only one hundred more shopping days till Christmas?" Kel guessed with a shrug.

"Just forget it. Look, we're going to practice layups. So you run towards the basket, then I'll pass you the ball and you lay it up. Got it?"

A sharp nod from Kel indicated that he did, indeed, have it. "I'm right on it!" he confirmed as he rushed towards the basket. He arched his head back over his shoulder, searching for the pass. Kenan sent the ball flying from his hands. It bounced onto the ground about halfway between him and Kel, then rebounded perfectly off of the court and landed right into Kel's arms. Kel tossed the ball up into the air towards the basket, and then made a crucial error. He forgot to stop running. Kel's face hit the metal pole with a loud metallic-sounding crack. His eyes rolled back into his eyelids, then, making a full rotation around the inside of his head, they reappeared at the bottom of his eyelids, crossed, and then shut altogether. Kel tipped backwards, like a giant tree that had just run into a far bigger metallic tree, and he crashed to the ground.

The ball, amazingly, dropped right through the net, with a quiet, whispering swish. It barely touched the nylon mesh at all as it fell straight through, landing right on top of Kel's upturned and unconscious face. It bounced up off of his face only to fall back down and land on his sleeping noggin again and again and again, before it finally seemed to tire of smacking Kel in the head, and rolled away in search of something better to do.

Something was wrong. Kel was sure of it. He wasn't able to fix on exactly what it was that wasn't right, but he had a strange feeling that it had something to do with the sharp, stinging pain that was dancing across his forehead, like a four-hundred-pound ballerina in high heels. He looked around.

Everything was dark. That also seemed a little odd to Kel. *This day is turning out very confusing,* Kel thought. Another sharp, ringing pain stung its way across Kel's head. *Man, all this thinking really hurts,* he thought, and winced as even that thought was accompanied by pain.

Wait! Something new seemed to be happening. He was hearing something. *Hopefully it's someone telling me what's going on,* Kel desperately hoped against hope.

It was a little clearer now, the voice. It was starting to make sense. It was a familiar voice.

"Kel! Kel!" Kenan yelled at his friend who lay sprawled out across the rough concrete of the court. A large red welt marked Kel's face, showing the shape of the pole that he had smacked into.

Kel's eyes fluttered. His head lolled slightly to the right, and then turned and lolled slightly to the left.

Wait! Something new is happening! thought Kel as Kenan grabbed him by the shoulders and began trying to shake him awake. *The ground has gone all shaky!* A wave of panic sprinted its way through his limp body. *Oh no! Earthquake!*

"Earthquake!" Kel shouted as his eyes flew open, and in one swift and entirely unexpected motion he leapt to his feet.

Kenan reeled back in surprise. His arms flailed out at his sides, fighting to keep his balance. He tripped over his feet and tumbled backwards to the ground.

"The world is coming to an end! Awwww, we're all gonna die!" Kel shouted to the sky.

"Man!" Kenan groaned, pulling himself slowly to his feet. "Kel, what are you yelling about?"

Kel stopped, his narrow face tilted up towards the clouds. His eyebrows scrunched together like they were fighting to shake hands over the bridge of his nose. Finally, he shrugged and looked over at his friend. "I don't know," he said with bubbly enthusiasm.

"What's going on, Kenan?"

"Well," he began, trying not to laugh as he spoke, but not having a lot of success at it. "You ran into that big pole there and knocked yourself out and you just been lying there all unconscious for like the past five minutes."

"Cool," Kel said, his head bobbing up and down in excitement.

Kenan's face sagged.

He sat down on the court, drew his knees up to his slumping chest, and quietly gave up. "Awww, I give up! This is no use. We're never gonna beat the McThunks! Who are we kidding?"

"Ourselves?" Kel offered.

A drop of sweat crept slowly down Kenan's face as he looked around at the playground. It was slowly starting to fill up with other kids at play. Happier kids. Kids who weren't about to face a humiliating basketball defeat for the second time in a week. Kenan sat watching the other children with quiet envy. They had no worries. And why should they? Come Monday, there was very little chance that any of them would be wearing shirts with the word "Loser" written across them in large, humiliating letters for all to see.

He began rocking slowly back and forth on the warm cement of the court. "It's just not fair," he squeaked to himself. The McThunks were bullies, and bullies weren't supposed to win. Bullies were supposed to lose. If countless hours in front of the television had taught Kenan anything it was that good guys win and bullies lose. And if he could no longer trust television, then what was his world coming to? What kind of world was it where—

"Hey, could you throw us our ball back?"

A basketball rolled past Kenan, but he didn't move. He was too lost in thought.

"Hey!" The call came again from across the court where a group of kids were gathered. "A little help here. Could you throw us back our ball?" A tall kid wearing bright red shorts that just about matched the shade of his bright red hair and his bright red sun-burned face looked eagerly down the court towards Kenan and Kel for a response.

Kenan didn't notice the basketball that had just rolled past him and was now coming to a stop right at Kel's feet.

Kel looked down at the ball. He looked back up at the group of kids dotting the other side of the court. Cupping a hand to his mouth, he yelled back to them, "What does your ball look like?"

The redheaded kid stared at Kel across the forty feet of court that stood between them. "Our ball looks like the one that's at your feet!" he screamed through the warm air.

Kel glanced down at the ball again. He had an idea. Picking it up he shouted across the court, "Hey, maybe this is your ball, since they look alike and everything."

The redheaded kid and his friends all nodded in answer to Kel's question.

"It's not like I'm a bad person," Kenan muttered, continuing his conversation with nobody. "I'm basically good. Mostly good anyway. Well, at least, sorta good," he rambled on, oblivious to the goings-on around him.

Kel held the ball in the palm of his hand. "Okay," he shouted, "here it comes." He arched back, dipped his shoulder, and with a series of muscular contractions that even he couldn't explain, he let the ball fly.

Kenan didn't see the ball as it left Kel's hand. He didn't watch as it sailed gracefully through the air. And, due to the fact that he was looking the other way, he didn't catch sight of it as it dropped, amazingly, through the net with a light, airy swish. What he did notice was the cheering.

They didn't cheer right away. The first thing that the redheaded kid and his friends did was stare in shock. First at the ball, then up at the basket. They turned to stare at Kel. That's when they started to cheer.

"All right! Nice shot!" shouted Red.

"Man, that was like, half-court!" a short, plump kid yelled.

"No," another friend disagreed. "Look at him. That was more than half-court. That was like, half-court plus."

Red snatched the ball from the ground and squeezed it firmly between his hands, staring at it in thought. Then, glancing up at Kel, he yelled, "Hey, try that again." And threw the ball back.

Kenan looked up from his spot on the ground as the ball landed back in Kel's hands. "What's going on?"

"Oh nothing," Kel answered innocently.

"Oh." Kenan shrugged and started to resume his rocking and mumbling and feeling bad for himself.

"I just made a basket in that hoop way over there, from way over here, that's all."

"Well, if that's all then—What!" Kenan was on his feet in a flash. He whirled around and looked at the other basket, so small in the distance. His finger shot out and pointed down the court. "There?" he exclaimed incredulously. "You got this ball in that basket way over there?!"

"Yep."

"No way!"

Kel shrugged, lifted up the ball and threw it again. Kenan's eyes followed the ball as it flew through the sky. Red and his three friends followed the ball as it flew through the sky. No one looked away. No one blinked. One person did belch, but even that didn't make him look away. And then . . . Swish! Unbelievably the ball dropped into the net for a second time.

Kenan's jaw dropped. He looked at Kel, then back at the basket, then back at Kel, then at his shoes, the basket, and Kel again in rapid, disbelieving succession. "What the—" he started, but that didn't seem quite right. "Would ya—" he tried again, but again he stopped. "With the—" He shook his head from side to side as he fought to complete a sentence. He was amazed. Kel had made that impossible shot, not once, but twice. Twice couldn't be a fluke. Could it? "Do it again," Kenan finally said.

Red and his three friends rushed over with the ball and surrounded Kel.

"That was awesome," Red gushed, his rosy cheeks flushing a little more red than usual from the excitement.

"Yeah, do it again!" the others chimed in, shoving the ball into Kel's arms.

"Well, I'll try." And again he threw the ball. Five heads turned in unison and watched as the ball landed right in the net.

The crowd burst into cheers and a flurry of high fives and back pats and friendly punches on the arm followed. All except for Kenan. He just stared at the ball. Somewhere, deep in the back of his eyes, a small glint had begun to glint. Deep inside his brain, thoughts were brewing. Hundreds of thousands of little brain cells snapped to attention as hundreds of thousands of brain cell reserves were called in to join the thinking.

"Let me try that!" Kenan stated as he marched across the court to retrieve the ball and quickly marched back. "That didn't look so hard." He hefted the ball up in his hand, feeling its weight. Judging it. His eyes narrowed to a steely glare as he eyed the hoop off in the distance. His arm muscles contracted and then relaxed in preparation for the big throw. Finally he hauled back and threw. CRASH!!

The windshield of the car shattered into a million tiny little windshield pieces as the ball smashed through it, coming to rest comfortably on the leather interior of the driver's seat. An ear-piercing alarm assaulted the air, blaring out from the damaged automobile to warn its owner that a ball was breaking in.

Kenan's eyes popped open. "Ooops," he murmured.

CHAPTER THREE

Rigby's Grocery would never be confused for a really nice grocery store. Really nice grocery stores had wide aisles stacked high with boxes of cereal and cans of soup and packages of instant liver paste that offered all the tasty goodness of real liver with the easy-to-chew convenience of a paste. Rigby's had no wide aisles, no tall shelves, and, sadly, though they carried a wide variety of products in paste form, liver paste was not one of them.

What Rigby's was, was a small, friendly, modest little grocery store. It had several small shelves with several small products on them. It had a modest dairy display with a very modest selection of milk and yogurt and assorted cheeses. And it had a friendly little deli counter where you could pick up a nice turkey or ham after a long, hard day of work. No, Rigby's may not have had the wide assortment of items that a nice big grocery store would have, but it did have one thing that other grocery stores didn't have. It had a pile of broken melons littering the floor.

"Man, that's unbelievable," Kenan marveled, shaking his head back and forth, high cheekbones standing out in amazment as he handed another ripe, round melon to Kel. Kenan was working extra hours at Rigby's to pay for the windshield damage. "Try it again from back here behind the counter."

Kel took the cantaloupe, absently running his hand over the hard, gray shell that protected the sweet orange fruit within. He climbed over the counter and pressed his back against the far wall.

A makeshift basket hung across from him over the glass front door of the market. The basket looked a lot like a trash can from which the bottom had been removed. It probably looked like that because only a half an hour before it had been a trash can, sitting in a forgotten corner of Rigby's. Kenan had grabbed it, turned it upside down, and yelled, "Hey, this will make a good basket, all I gotta do is punch the bottom out." The trash can didn't know who Kenan was or what a basket was, or why it had to have its bottom punched out for that matter. In fact the trash can didn't really think anything, because after all, it was just a trash can and trash cans can't think.

Kerthunk! The basket rattled noisily against the metal door frame as Kel launched another melon in a perfect arc across the room and dropped it into the basket with pinpoint precision. The melon thunked off the sides of the former trash can, then slipped through the newly opened bottom and dropped to the tile floor. It cracked open lying side by side with a small pile of other melons that had also recently met the same fate.

"Man! Another one." Kenan curled up next to the lone cash register, pulling his feet up next to him as he sat on the counter watching the show. A small, perplexing grin seemed frozen on his face. "I don't get it, Kel, how do you do it?"

"Oh, it's easy. See, all I do is judge the distance between me and the basket." Kel scratched at his chin knowledgeably. "Then I simply gauge the appropriate force needed to carry the ball to the basket, taking into consideration, of course, the constant force of gravity acting against it."

Kenan cocked his head to one side. "Uh-huh." He nodded along skeptically at Kel's explanation. "That was very impressive, Kel, but do you actually know what any of that stuff you just said means?"

"No," Kel replied weakly, hanging his head against his chest. "I just thought that it sounded better than the truth."

"Well what's the truth then?" Kenan asked, his voice thick with the anticipation of an even goofier answer. He knew Kel very well, and Kel could always be counted on for a goofy answer. Once again, he didn't disappoint.

"I just clear my mind of everything until it's completely blank."

"Man, your mind is always completely blank! Ha!" Kenan laughed at his own little joke as he hopped down off of the counter, walked over to Kel, and slapped him on his back to share in the funny.

A thought struck Kenan and he stopped laughing and stared at his friend questioningly for a moment.

"What?" Kel asked, paranoid. He lifted his lips and rubbed at his teeth with his finger. "Do I have something in my teeth? Is there something in my nose? What are you looking at?" His voice rose as he tried to figure out what hideous and grotesque facial deformation Kenan was staring at.

A look of confusion had perched itself on Kenan's face. "I'm not looking at anything," he began slowly, curiously. "I was just wondering something." He was about to let Kel know exactly what it was that he had been wondering, but before he got the chance, Kel cut him off.

"Ohhh, were you wondering how come there is no such thing as foot deodorant?"

"Uh . . . no." Kenan felt his facial muscles begin to clench ever so slightly in that special way that only Kel could make them clench.

"Ohhh, I know." Kel hopped excitedly from foot to foot as he eagerly took another guess. "Were you wondering—"

Kenan's hand shot into the air like a spring. "Stop right there. No," he answered.

"But, you don't know what I was gonna ask."

"But I'm sure the answer's no," Kenan responded with the absolute confidence of someone who had heard Kel be wrong about a whole lot of things over the years. "Now, what I was gonna say was, if you can make all these shots, then how come we lost so badly to the McThunks? You couldn't make any shot then."

Kel shrugged his shoulders up against his ears and held them there. "I don't know. I guess I'm just not very good at those close-up shots."

"Hey fellas, I'm back from dropping Mother off at the heavy metal concert."

Kenan's eyes popped open wide. He knew immediately whom that warm and nasally voice belonged to. And he knew immediately what that voice meant. Trouble.

Trouble, in this case, rounded the corner in the form of Kenan's boss, Chris Potter. Chris was about average height and average weight and average age, but that was all that was average about Chris's appearance. His thick, dark head of hair was sprayed into a thick solid fortress of follicles that guarded the top of his head. His longer than average face framed a slightly larger than average nose, and an even larger, lopsided grin. A lopsided grin that quickly vanished as soon as Chris pushed his way into his store.

He stopped and his face plummeted towards the ground as he got a look at the mess of discarded fruit that littered the floor in front of him. A small tic in the corner of his eye began to twitch uncontrollably, jittering around under the skin like a stoplight gone berserk.

Finally, muscular control worked its way back down his face from the small twitch to his mouth. "What happened here?" He actually took a step back as he said it to better take in the melon carnage that lay strewn across the tile floor of his store like a mighty melon army that had lost a great battle to an apparently much better and tougher army of some better and tougher fruit. His eyes shot up and locked onto Kenan's nervous face. "I thought I told you to stack the melons," Chris demanded accusingly as he began to inch forward towards his wayward employee.

Kenan backed up nervously. His eyes darted from side to side. His lip quivered slightly. Even his hair looked a little more nervous than dreadlocks usually managed to look. "Uh . . . see . . . uh . . . Chris," he stuttered as he searched deep into the hidden recesses of his brain for an excuse. "Uh . . ." His hands flailed through the air like a couple of birds that had lost the ability to navigate and ended up just flying in demented, jumpy circles through the sky. "Uh . . . oh, you said stack the melons?" he asked as his back began to press up against the counter. "Oh, see, 'cause I thought you said, 'Smash the melons all over the floor.' Oops. Heh heh."

"Kenan!" Chris barked at him angrily. "Just . . . clean this up before someone slips on it and hurts themself!"

Kel, who had been quietly watching the whole scene unfold in front of him, finally joined in. "Yeah right, Chris." He laughed. "Like that would really happen."

The words had no sooner slipped out of Kel's mouth when a soft ringing at the door announced that a customer was entering. The ringing of the bell was quickly replaced by a yelp of surprise as the customer stepped onto the moist and mushy pile of melons. His surprised customer feet slipped on the moist fruit, sending him skittering and sliding across the floor. His short customer arms pinwheeled wildly at his thick customer side, until finally, with a high-pitched yell for help, he collided with the front counter, tumbled over it, and disappeared from sight with a loud, painful-sounding crash.

Kel casually sauntered over to the counter and peered over it, staring down at the customer on the other side. With an arch of his eyebrow and a shrug, Kel conceded, "Hey, what do you know, Chris, you were right." Kel shot Chris two big thumbs-up and tipped a friendly wink in his direction.

Chris narrowed his eyes and shook his head sadly from side to side.

A thought struck Kenan. A warm and fuzzy and happy thought that made his brain tingle and sent chills down his spine. His eyes darted from the melons to the basket and then over to Kel. The edges of his lips leapt upwards towards his eyes and his cheeks flushed with a rosy glow of excitement. He clutched Kel by the shoulders and squeezed. "Kel, do you know what this means?" he asked, his voice light and eager.

"Yeah, Chris is gonna have to pay for that guy's doctor bills," Kel answered.

"No!" he said, then stopped and craned his neck to peer at the wreckage of the customer piled up on the other side of the counter. Then, with a shrug, he continued. "Well, actually, you and I are going to have to work even more hours now, but that's not what I'm talking about."

"What are you talking about?"

Kenan's eyes were fiery with excitement and they burned into Kel as he spoke. "I'm talking about basketball, Kel. I'm talking about the McThunks! And I'm talking about winning!"

"Ohhhhh!" Kel nodded along enthusiastically, smiling broadly at Kenan's plan. Then his smile quickly dropped. "What are you talking about?" he asked, confused.

Kenan took a deep breath and let it out slowly. Even Kel couldn't upset him right now. Because Kenan had a plan.

CHAPTER FOUR

Roger Rockmore was not a little man. His father had not been a little man. Even his grandfather had not been a little man.

Even with the history of his large family members, Kenan's dad was still large by comparison. His arms were large, his legs were large, his chest was large, even his small intestine was large. And his large intestine . . . well, that just goes without saying. Roger Rockmore stood well over six feet tall. And perched at the top of that tall frame was a glowing bald head, that only managed to keep itself from looking frightening by the bright friendly smile that lit up its otherwise intimidating countenance. He was, despite his appearance, a pretty nice guy.

He was also, at the moment, a pretty hungry guy. Which was too bad for him, since he was currently on a diet. The diet was not his idea, it had actually been suggested by his wife, Sheryl, who had detected a few extra pounds loitering around Roger's middle. Roger had tried to insist to his wife that he didn't need to diet.

Those extra pounds were probably just friends of the pounds that were already living around his middle, and he was sure that once they were done visiting, they would be on their fatty ways all by themselves without having to resort to anything as drastic as a diet. Sheryl, of course, would have none of it. And so the diet had begun. That meant healthy, low-calorie meals that tasted, to Roger, as if they were made out of Styrofoam covered with dirt. It also meant no snacking between meals, which was what right now happened to be: between meals.

Roger rubbed soothingly at his grumbling belly. He looked towards the kitchen door, eyeing the food that was safely stored away beyond it.

Technically it wasn't really between meals, thought Roger. It was more before a meal. Sure it was five o'clock, and a lot of people may have considered that to fall somewhere "in between" lunch and dinner. But Roger had a different view of it. It wasn't in between lunch and dinner. In between lunch and dinner had been somewhere around three or four o'clock. No, right now was definitely not "in between" anything, it was simply before dinner. And Sheryl hadn't said anything about before meal snacks being off limits.

Just a little snack, he assured himself as he approached the refrigerator. *A small snack won't hurt anything.*

The sandwich stood about two feet off the table. Layer upon layer of pure food was stacked on more layers beneath them. It was like the Empire State Building of sandwiches. Except that instead of a towering structure of wrought iron and steel, this man-made edifice was constructed of bread and ham and mustard, cheese, relish, pickles, lettuce, tomato, mayonnaise, cucumbers, more cheese, hot sauce, green peppers, and a small dash of vinegar. But other than that, they were almost identical. The top layer of bread swayed gently from side to side as it tried to maintain its balance perched atop the stack of meats and breads that stood beneath it.

Roger lowered his head to stare at the sandwich eye to lunch meat. His deep-set eyes were round and wide in an expression of love and joy as he stared at his creation.

With one trembling hand, he gently stroked the bread on top. His mouth hung open slightly, anticipating the glorious moment when sandwich and taste buds would shake hands before getting down to some serious bonding.

Slowly and reverentially, Roger wrapped his hands around the massive mound of food and lifted it towards his mouth. His thick tongue danced from side to side, barely able to contain its tonguelike enthusiasm as it watched the sandwich approach with growing glee.

His mouth opened wide, then, seeing how enormous the sandwich was, opened even wider. His teeth glinted in the yellow kitchen light as—

"Daddy!" a voice scolded from the back kitchen door.

Roger froze. The sandwich lingered inches from his face, the sweet glorious scent of lunch meat danced around his nostrils as his eyes slowly turned to the back door to see . . .

Kyra. Kenan's sister. Roger's daughter. His youngest child. His special, precious little girl for whom he would do anything in the world if she asked him.

"Go away!" he snapped at her. "I'm busy."

She stepped into the room and pulled the door shut behind her.

"Yeah, busy breaking your diet. Now put that sandwich down." Kyra was twelve years old, but something in her voice caused her father to hesitate. He started to lower the sandwich, but stopped. He couldn't. It looked too good. It smelled too good. And he was just positive that it would taste too good. He had to have it. His hands trembled as the weight of the decision rested heavily on them.

"I can't. I'm so hungry," he moaned. "Must eat sandwich." A demonic glare lit up his eyes as he stared at the sandwich. "Now go away!" he barked.

Kyra didn't move. She just squared off against her dad with a cocky look. Roger's head and her own were almost level as he sat, and she met his shaky and hungry eyes with a confident and commanding stare of her own. They were squaring off over a large and impressively tasty looking sandwich.

"Put the sandwich down." She enunciated each word clearly and carefully, never taking her eyes from his.

"I can't!"

Then, Kyra pulled out her ace in the hole. "I'll tell Mom."

"You—you wouldn't?" he stammered. She had him and she knew it. And what's more, he knew she knew it. Which was just fine with her, because she knew that he knew that she knew it.

"Just put the sandwich down, and slide it over to me and no one will have to know," she ordered calmly through her braces.

With trembling hands, Roger set his culinary masterpiece down on the table in front of him and slowly, with great agony, slid it away from himself.

The kitchen door swung open with a gentle swish and Kenan and Kel entered the room.

"Hey, Rockmores!" Kel greeted Roger and Kyra with a yell.

"Hey, Pop. Hey, Kyra," Kenan acknowledged, which was more than his sister did for him. Ignoring Kenan completely, Kyra rushed over to Kel and glanced up at him through wide, love-struck, puppy-dog eyes.

"Hi, Kel," she gushed with a sigh.

Kel looked around nervously as Kyra stared up at him lovingly, batting her eyes in his direction.

"Kenan, your sister's looking at me all funny again."

Kenan put two hands on his sister's shoulders and gently moved her away from Kel. "Kyra, leave the boy alone. We've got some planning to discuss."

Roger eyed the sandwich that lay, tantalizingly, just across the table from him. He breathed the sandwich odor deep into his lungs. Now was his chance. Kyra was distracted. No one was watching. All he had to do was grab the sandwich. It was right there waiting for him. It was—

"Hey, sandwich!" Kel scooped up the sandwich in one hand and took a huge bite. Roger's face froze.

Kel chomped loudly on the large lunch, stuffing it, one large bite at a time, down into his mouth. In no time, it was all gone. Kel licked at his fingers, making sure to get every last drop of sandwich juice into his belly. "Mmmmmmmm-mmmm. That was one tasty sandwich."

Roger's lips quivered. His sandwich was gone forever.

"I mean," Kel continued, "I've had a lot of sandwiches before, but that one was just about the best sandwich I've ever had. It was just so good. It was like my stomach died and went to sandwich heaven. In fact, I don't think I'll ever taste anything quite that amazingly delicious ever again as long as I live."

Roger's hands began to tremble.

"Got it, Kel," Kenan said. "It's a good sandwich."

Kel put his hand out to stop Kenan. "Nah, nah, nah, Kenan. It wasn't just a good sandwich. It was a great sandwich. It was—"

Roger couldn't take it anymore. He sprung up out of his chair and bolted from the room, screaming a loud "Ahhhhhhhhhhhhhh!" as he went.

Three pairs of eyes watched Roger rush away. "Sheeesh, what's his problem?" Kel wondered aloud for all of them.

"Hey, Kel?" Kyra asked sweetly. "Wanna see something neat?"

Kel didn't seem terribly sure of how to answer, and finally, after several moments of hemming and hawing, he came out with a tentative, "Yeah?"

"Okay, watch. This is something I learned in school today." Kyra stood in front of him and held her arms out wide. Then, without warning, she rushed into Kel and locked her arms tightly around his back, grabbing him in a bear hug. She pressed her face into his chest and held on tight.

"Ack!" Kel acked. "Kenan, your sister's squeezing me again. She's crushing my liver!"

Kenan sighed, grabbed his sister's hands, and pried them apart. "Now go on, Kyra, get out of here. Kel and I have some planning to discuss."

Kyra pushed her bottom lip out in a pout, "Fine!"

she grumbled. "Bye, Kel!" she said hopefully and then, when he didn't answer, she pushed her way through the swinging door and out of the kitchen.

Kel shook his head as he watched her leave. "I can't believe they taught her that in school."

Kenan briefly considered explaining to Kel that no one had taught Kyra that in school, but he quickly decided that he had more important things to discuss. So he sat Kel down across from him at the table and began to discuss them.

"Never mind about that, Kel. Now listen up, we've got to go back down to that playground today and challenge those McThunks again."

"But, Kenan, we're not supposed to play them until Friday."

"I know that. But why wait until then? With your amazing half-court shot, we can't lose. Besides, if we go today, we'll catch them off-guard," Kenan explained. "Now here's the plan. Every time we get the ball, you just go back to the half-court line. No one's gonna guard you way back there. Then, I'll throw the ball to you, you throw it into the basket, and we win."

"I don't know, Kenan." Kel shook his head with concern. "How am I supposed to make a shot from way back there?"

Kenan narrowed his eyes as he stared at his friend in wonder. It was amazing that Kel managed to function in the everyday world when he was capable of saying things as ridiculous as that.

"Kel, you've been making that shot all day long. You haven't missed once."

Kel thought about it for a moment. "Oh, yeah." He grinned. "Good plan, Kenan."

Sheryl Rockmore, Kenan's mom, walked into the

kitchen, an excited look lighting up her slender, pretty features. She ran a hand through the short, fashionable hair that framed her friendly face. "Kenan?" she asked as soon as she saw her son. "Have you seen your father?"

"Yeah," Kel interjected helpfully, "he's the big, bald guy."

"Thank you, Kel." She tried to remain polite, but sometimes Kel made it so difficult. "I meant, do you know where he is? I've got a surprise for him."

"Oh. I think he's upstairs crying about some sandwich or something," Sheryl's son answered with a shrug.

"Oh, poor Roger. This diet has been so hard on him. But I have just the thing to cheer him up."

"Hair?" Kel asked sincerely.

Sheryl bit her lip. "No, Kel, not hair. I got us two tickets to the Bulls game tomorrow night."

Kenan wasn't really paying attention. He was too busy envisioning their great basketball victory against the dreaded McThunks. He formed a mental picture in his mind of Billy's gigantic head lolling sadly towards the ground as the humiliation of playground defeat weighed heavily upon it. Kenan smiled. It was a very happy picture.

"Well, that's great and all, Mom," he said, "but me and Kel got stuff to do. Come on, Kel, to the playground! It's show time."

"McThunks!" Kenan yelled into the clear playground air. All activity stopped suddenly. Every swing stopped swinging. Every seesaw stopped seesawing. Every jungle gym stopped jungle-gymming, as all eyes turned to gawk at Kenan.

Kenan held his head up high as the sun bathed him in a warm, victorious glow. He was feeling very, very good. "McThunks!" he shouted again. For a brief moment he was answered only with the still sound of shocked silence coming from all the other kids on the playground. They had seen some crazy things in their days, but nothing as crazy as someone actually calling out to the McThunks. This was sure to go down in playground history, to be handed down to future playground generations as something never to do.

Then the silence was broken by the soft sound of snorting laughter in the distance.

Kenan and Kel stood shoulder to shoulder, basketball firmly clenched in hand as the laughter grew closer. They looked from side to side at all the frozen faces, watching, and all the abandoned playground equipment, sitting still and unused. They couldn't see the McThunks anywhere. But there was no mistaking that laugh. It was a low, animal kind of snort that could send shivers up the spine of even the bravest basketball players. And it got louder, closer. It seemed all around them, like the air itself was snorting. And then it was joined by another noise. A quick, sharp laugh. *Ha ha ha ha ha ha ha. Snort, snort, snort.* Together they sounded like the worst symphony in the world.

"What you got there, Rockmore?" The voice was directly behind them. Kenan and Kel jumped and whirled around in surprise. There, standing directly in front of them were the McThunks. Billy leered out at them from his huge head. Brian's jagged smile stretched out across the length of his face with a cruel sort of glee. Their shadows loomed across the short length of court between them and Kenan and Kel, darkening the asphalt.

Kenan swallowed hard. Suddenly his brilliant plan didn't seem to be such a good idea. The crowds of playground patrons inched their way towards the court. They knew that whatever was about to happen was something that they didn't want to miss.

Kenan tried to keep the nervous trembling that he felt in his gut out of his voice as he looked Billy straight in the eyes and said, "Let's play. First to eleven wins. Losers wear the loser shirts for a whole week."

The brothers didn't even bother to answer. They merely looked at each other. Then they snatched the ball out of Kenan's hands and marched back to the half-court line to take it in.

Billy held the ball up next to his own globe-sized noggin. They were about the same size. "Check," he growled, and threw the ball towards Kenan, hard.

The throw caught Kenan off-guard, and before he had a chance to react, the ball smacked him in the chest and dropped to the ground. Kenan was a little flustered, which was exactly Billy's plan. Intimidation and flustering always played a big role in their success. Finally, Kenan grabbed the ball off the ground and threw it back to his nemesis. "Check," he responded weakly, and the game was on.

Brian danced around the court as Kel tried to guard him; finally he sprinted free of Kel and Billy shot a perfectly timed pass right into his brother's open arms. Kenan rushed up under the basket to try to prevent Brian from scoring. But as soon as Kenan made his move, Brian faked a shot, pumping his arms towards the basket, then pulling them back in and passing the ball like a bullet over to Billy, who was now open for an easy outside jump shot. The ball rebounded off the backboard and dropped right into the net. McThunks: 1; Kenan and Kel: 0.

Billy pushed his face right into Kenan's as he recovered the ball. "Ha!" he snorted, and dribbled the ball back to the line to take it in again.

Brian raced around the court, trying to get open, but this time Kenan and Kel were both covering him. He couldn't break free. Unfortunately that meant that Billy was completely open, and he didn't waste the opportunity. He sprinted forward, unopposed to the basket, for an easy layup. Two to nothing.

Billy to Brian to Billy and back to Brian. He shoots, he scores. Three to nothing.

"Kenan, was this part of your plan?" Kel asked nervously as Billy took the ball out once again.

Kenan shrugged then grimaced. "Not exactly."

Billy eyed the court, waiting for his brother to get open. But this time Kel was sticking right with him. Kenan was busy putting on pressure of his own, waving his hands high in the air in front of Billy's face.

Pumpkin Head went to jump, but Kenan was right on him. He leapt into the air, hands up to block the pass, but it was a fake. McThunk shot the ball down low, rebounding off the ground towards his brother. Kel saw the pass and swung his arms towards it as it approached. He grabbed for it, hands outstretched, but he just missed it, smacking it away instead. Kenan went for the ball as it rolled, bouncing across the court on its own, but Billy got there first, snatching the ball out of the air, spinning around Kenan, and tossing the ball up into the air where his brother's waiting hands grabbed it and slammed it home. Four to zip.

It seemed that no matter what they did, no matter how hard they tried, Kenan and Kel just couldn't get the ball. The brothers were just too good. It was five, nothing and then six and seven. Billy and Brian dunked, they shot from outside, from inside, layups, jumpers, eight, nothing, nine, nothing. And then, just when it looked like it was all over, just as the playground spectators began to wander off, not having the stomachs to witness such a brutal beating, something happened. Kel tripped.

Now Kel tripping may not seem like such a good thing to have happen, but considering that while Kel was on his feet, things weren't going so well either, it couldn't really make it any worse. Kel happened to stumble over his own feet and crash to the ground, just as Brian was about to shoot. The smaller McThunk, for just the briefest, most minuscule of moments, glanced down to watch Kel hit the ground. And that's all it took. His shot was just a little off. It hit the rim of the basket and bounced away, landing right into Kenan's surprised hands. Billy saw what happened and stormed across the court towards Kenan, thick hands waving above his planet-sized head.

Kenan shot the ball down low, bouncing it expertly under Billy's tree-trunk-sized legs.

Kel was just pulling himself to his feet as the ball bounded towards him.

"Back to half-court! Back to half-court!" Kenan shrieked.

Brian recovered from his poor shot and began to move towards Kel for the steal. And then Kel did something surprising. Instead of heading towards the basket, Kel ran away, dribbling the ball in front of him.

Before Brian could figure out what was going on, Kel stepped back to the half-court line, just an inch shy of stepping out of bounds. As the two McThunks finally reacted and began thundering their way towards him, Kel threw the ball into the air. It arched high into the sky, its shadow getting smaller and then larger on the court as it began to fall back towards the ground. *Thwick!* The net flipped up as the ball dropped through.

One to nine.

Kel took the ball out. Kenan sprinted long towards the basket with Billy hot on his heels. Kel took one step in bounds and threw the ball. SCORE! Two to nine.

He did it again, and again, a perfect shot. Four to nine.

The playground audience that had begun to walk away returned quickly with a buzz. The air almost seemed to hum with excitement as the score changed from four, then five, then six, then seven to nine. Something that every kid on that playground hoped to witness but never dared to dream was actually happening. The McThunks, after years of playground terror, might actually lose.

But the brothers in question weren't about to give up that easily. They were still ahead nine to seven. It was still their game to lose. All they had to do was get the ball back. They huddled up as Kel took the ball back out of bounds. Billy's head bobbed up and down threateningly as he laid out his plan to his little brother.

This time as Kel took the ball out, both brothers rushed up to him, hands and heads in the air in front of his face, blocking his view and his shot. Kel searched for an opening among the blur of hands and arms and fingers and heads in front of his face. He stepped forward and shot. *Smack!* The ball hit Billy in the forehead and bounced straight up into the air. Kenan, Kel, and Brian looked up as the ball went straight up into the sky. Billy rubbed his head with a thick paw and then looked up as well. All eyes in the crowd followed the ball. All four players huddled together waiting for it to come back down, arms ready to grab, and legs ready to spring.

It began to drop. A hush fell over the entire field, the entire block, maybe even the entire city, as the ball began its descent.

Billy jumped first, stretching his arms upward towards the ball. He was quick. Lightning quick. Just a millisecond quicker than his little brother, who also managed to get into the air before Kenan or Kel.

Billy got his meaty hooks around the ball. A broad smile spilled across his chin, somehow managing to be dwarfed by the immensity of the rest of his head. This was it and he knew it. The game was theirs. They were going to win. They—*crack!!!*

It was a loud noise, as if a meteorite had struck a planet. The meteorite in question happened to be the head of Brian McThunk, and the planet it crashed into was the head of Billy McThunk.

The crowd winced. Not that they felt bad for the brothers, but it sounded that awful.

Billy dropped the ball, which landed right into Kenan's arms. He dribbled towards the basket as the two brothers came crashing down into a tangled mountain of pain. Kenan dribbled up under the basket and easily laid the ball in.

The crowd was hushed. No one moved. No one breathed. All eyes were locked on the pile of McThunks. They were lying still and silent. Then in one quick twitch, they moved! The whole crowd jumped back, like an audience in a horror movie that thought the killer was done for but who were clearly mistaken.

The bad brothers staggered to their feet, wobbling on weak knees as they stood.

"You know, if you guys want to quit, that's okay," Kenan offered as he walked up to them.

"Blemin hahhhhhh!" Billy shouted, dazed and angry.

"I guess that's a 'no,' huh?" Kenan asked, then added, "Okay! Kel, take it out again." And that's exactly what Kel did.

"Eight to nine." Kenan kept score as they went.

"Nine to nine," he reported as Kel landed another shot over the heads of the wobbly brothers.

"Op! Looks like that's ten to nine," Kenan taunted. "That's game point."

The McThunks tried to concentrate, to shake the confusion out of their bruised and swelling heads. They had to stop this shot. A steely glint sparked up in the back of Brian's deep-set eyes. A determined sort of spark. The sort of spark that would not admit defeat, that would play till the end. The sort of spark that would win. Then, as quickly as it had come, the spark went out.

Kel stepped in bounds and shot. The game was won. The McThunks wobbled, staggered, and then collapsed to the ground as the crowd erupted into cheers, storming onto the court to congratulate Kenan and Kel. They had done the unthinkable. They had brought the McThunks' reign of playground terror to an end. Kenan and Kel had won.

CHAPTER FIVE

Kenan's smile stretched across his face and stole its way up his cheeks and towards his ears. His eyes beamed brilliantly the way only the eyes of someone who had recently become a playground hero can beam. He stared off into space, replaying the great and glorious day over and over again in his mind. It had been perfect.

Kel sat next to him on the couch, matching his smile almost size for size. There were only two slight differences between Kel's smile and that of his friend. First, there was the small gap between Kel's front teeth. And, second, Kel's smile seemed to be tinted a little orange. Maybe the flush of victory had rushed to his lips and turned them a bright shade of orange. But more likely the staining around his mouth had something to do with the discarded bottles of orange soda that lay strewn across the floor around him.

Kel lifted a last bottle of orange soda to his lips and in one loud, wet gulp, he downed it. The clear plastic bottle dropped to the floor and took its place among its clear plastic brethren. Kel belched a rattling orangy belch for good measure. The smell of orange filled the air and Kenan winced as it crawled its way up into his nose.

"Aw man, that's nasty!" he complained to his friend.

"No it's not. It's orange soda," Kel replied.

Kenan shook his head as he turned on the TV. As the picture shimmied into view in front of them, the announcer's voice broke over the speaker. "We'll be right back to start our movie, *Revenge of the Blood-Sucking Monkeys,* after these messages."

Kel's head snapped up to attention. "Hey, Kenan, did you hear that? *Revenge of the Blood-Sucking Monkeys* is on next."

Kenan had heard and was busily nodding along in excitement. "I know. I love that movie."

"It's, like, one of the best movies ever made," Kel stated with glee as visions of monkeys eating bananas and getting revenge danced feverishly through his brain.

"I know! Man, this day is amazing. Everything just keeps getting better and better. I bet nothing can top this."

The picture on the TV faded to black and then faded up on footage of the Chicago Bulls slammin' the ball home.

"Hey look at that, Kel." Kenan jabbed his finger towards the television. "That looks like us out there today."

"I don't know," Kel responded skeptically. "We weren't wearing uniforms."

Kenan glanced over at his friend. "Nah, I just meant that . . . Ah, never mind."

"Tomorrow on WGBC," the announcer's deep baritone voice burst through the airwaves, "the Chicago Bulls take on the Orlando Magic, live. And at halftime, five lucky fans will get to try their luck at a half-court free throw shot for five thousand dollars."

Kenan's ears stood up and took notice. He leaned forward to listen closer.

"It's half-court at halftime," the announcer continued in his booming dramatic voice. "But you gotta be there to win, so get your tickets now at 1-800-TICKET. Bulls, Magic, and you."

As the sound faded away, Kenan's eyes grew big. His eyebrows arched up in a dramatic arch stretching towards his hairline. He looked like a mad scientist, whose horrible mad scientist creation has just come to life. He rose, slowly, to his feet.

"Kel, did you hear that?"

Kel nodded. "Yeah, you just said, 'Kel, did you hear that?'"

Kenan waved his hands in front of Kel's face. "No!" he snapped with a hint of frustration. "Didn't you just hear what they said on the TV? Five lucky fans are gonna get to try a half-court free throw shot at tomorrow's game for five thousand dollars."

Kel didn't seem impressed. "So," he said nonchalantly. "I don't see what that has to do with me."

Kenan shook his head back and forth, then back and forth again. "You don't see what that has to do with you?! Kel, what have you been doing all day long?"

"Breathing?"

"No! Well, yeah, but that's not what I'm talking about. I'm talking about you making half-court free throw shots all day long. And now, on this greatest day of our entire lives, this day where everything has worked out right for us, we hear that they are gonna give five thousand dollars if someone can make a half-court shot at tomorrow night's Bulls game, and you don't see what that has to do with you?"

Kel took in all of what Kenan was saying, and then with a curt nod, replied, "Yep, that about sums it up."

Kenan was pacing back and forth in front of his seated friend. He rubbed his hands together in front of him as he pondered what he had done right to make fate smile so brightly on him today. "Kel, don't you see? It's like a sign."

"Nah, I think it was just a commercial for the Bulls game."

Kenan stopped and knelt down in front of Kel. He extended one arm and rested it on his friend's shoulder. "Kel," he began patiently. "You and me have to go to that game. Then we have to make sure that you are one of the five fans picked from the audience, and then you have to make that half-court shot. It's fate."

Kel's mouth creased up into a nervous, worried sort of frown. "I don't know. I mean, how are we gonna get to that game?"

Kenan stood. He hadn't thought that far yet, but now his every thought, his every fiber, was devoted to—"Hey, wait a minute. My parents have tickets!" he exclaimed. "So, all we have to do is get them to give their tickets to us."

"How are we gonna get them to do that?"

Kenan looked around the room as he thought. "I'm not sure yet, but give me some time, I'll figure it out."

Unfortunately time was something that Kenan was not about to get a lot of, because at exactly that moment, the front door opened and in walked his parents and his sister.

"Sheryl!" Roger groaned as he followed his wife into the house. "Please can't I get something to eat! I'm sooo hungry." He clutched his hands together in front of himself pleadingly.

"No, Roger. Now quit your whining."

"Mother, Father," Kenan's face lit up as he turned to face his family. "So lovely to see you."

"Nice to see you, too, Kenan," Kyra responded. "What do you want?"

Kenan grandly made his way across the room. "Ah, dear sister, aren't you funny. Now run along! Mom and Dad and I have something to discuss." He shoved Kyra to the side and stepped up in front of his parents. Kyra immediately shot back in front of her brother and glared up at him with suspicious twelve-year-old eyes.

"What are you up to, Kenan?" Her gaze bored into his head as if she could read his mind.

"Uh . . . nothing," her brother stammered nervously. "Up to? Me? Nothing at all. Hey, I got an idea! Why don't you go sit with Kel."

"Okay!" she blurted out, all suspicions of her brother forgotten, at least momentarily. She sprinted across the room, vaulted over the couch, and landed right in Kel's lap. "Hi, Kel," she gushed without missing a beat.

"Hi," Kel responded uncomfortably. "I think you just broke my lap."

She slapped him playfully on the chest. "Oh, you're so funny."

Roger and Sheryl tried to step farther into their nicely furnished living room but they were blocked.

Kenan was standing right in front of them, right between them and the couch and the cozy chair that Roger liked to sit in, and of course the TV that sat against the outside wall of the large, comfortable room like a shrine.

Sheryl shot an irritated glance at her son. "Can we do something for you?"

"Nah, well, you know, not really," Kenan said. "I was just doing some thinking about my birthday and all."

"Your birthday?" Roger asked, his booming voice laced with frustration and hunger.

Kenan nervously forged ahead. "Yeah, you know it's coming up and all and I was just thinking that you guys shouldn't have to go and buy me some expensive gift or anything."

Sheryl arched her eyebrows. She knew her son well enough to be suspicious of his motives. "Really?" she asked in a voice laced with doubt.

"Yeah," Kenan continued, desperately fighting to sound sincere. "I was thinking that you could just give me something that you already had. You know, maybe something in your pocket or something."

Roger had had enough, he pushed his way past his son. "What are you talking about?" he demanded.

Kenan felt the whole thing slipping away from him. He couldn't ask for the tickets now. His parents were in too bad a mood. He had to think quickly, he had to get them back on his good side first and then hit them up for the tickets. But what could he do? He was losing them, and fast. He could feel it. He had to think quickly.

"You know what?" he announced loudly. "You guys look hungry and tired. Why don't you let me make dinner for you tonight." He stopped and eyed his parents closely to see how they would take it.

At the first mention of dinner, Roger stopped and looked up. He licked at his lips hungrily. Kenan had him. But what about his mom? Nothing registered on her face. It was hard to tell how she took it. Then, finally, she spoke.

"Kenan, that is really nice of you. Thank you." She gave him a quick peck on the top of the head. She was his. There was only one little problem left to face. Kenan didn't know how to cook.

"Great, then. You guys just sit down and make yourselves comfortable and I'm just gonna go in the kitchen and try to . . . figure out how to cook . . . something."

Roger and Sheryl slumped down into their chairs as Kenan made his way across the living room, past the dining room table, and over to the swinging door that led to the kitchen. "Pssst. Kel," he hissed at his friend. "Come here."

"Okay!" Kel yelped excitedly and jumped to his feet, spilling Kyra off his lap and onto the floor.

"Hey!" she complained from the rug where she landed. She pulled herself to her feet and stormed angrily out of the room.

"What's up, Kenan?" Kel asked as he approached.

Kenan looked from side to side as if to make sure no one was listening in. They weren't. "Look," he began in a conspiratorial whisper. "I'm gonna try and figure out how to cook something. While I do, you do something nice for my parents. We have to get them on our good side if we're gonna get those tickets from them."

Kel nodded. He understood. "Got it."

Kenan gave one last uncertain glance at his friend, then shrugged and pushed his way into the kitchen.

Sheryl leaned back in the chair and stretched her slender arms high above her head. "Well," she said as she stood up, "I think I'm gonna take a bath while he's making dinner."

Do something nice. Do something nice. Kenan's words ran around Kel's head. They had plenty of room to run, since there wasn't much else occupying the space. He saw his opportunity and he jumped in.

"Do you need some help?" he offered.

Sheryl's head snapped around in surprise. "What?!" she exclaimed.

Roger's head also shot up from the reclined position where it lay. "What did you say?" he demanded.

Kel's shoulders sagged. His eyes darted around nervously. His tongue suddenly seemed thicker than a tongue should normally be. "Uh . . ." he faltered. "I was just trying to do something nice."

"Well, thank you, Kel, but I can manage on my own." Sheryl shook her head, turned, and marched up the stairs that sat against the back wall.

Kel watched her go, then turned back to face Mr. Rockmore, who was busy glaring at him.

"You want to really do something nice?" Roger asked him. "How about leave."

Kel thought about it, then shook his head. "I don't think that counts."

"It does for me," Roger insisted.

Kel's mind raced, he tried to think of something nice to do for Mr. Rockmore. There had to be something. The poor bald-headed man looked so stressed out. *Hey, wait a minute,* he thought, *that's it.*

"Hey, Mr. Rockmore," Kel said as he maneuvered

himself around behind Roger's chair. "You look a little tense. Why don't I give you a nice back rub."

"No, Kel, I don't want a—"

But Kel wasn't taking no for an answer. He grabbed a hold of Roger's shoulders with two firm grips and began squeezing.

"Ah! Ah! Ah!" Roger squealed in pain. "Would you get off of my back." He reached behind him and swatted at Kel with a thick, muscular arm. Kel managed to duck and dodge his swipes, all the while continuing with the brutal massage.

"Ohhh, you are tense!" Kel jabbered away like a gossipy hairdresser. He decided that just rubbing wasn't gonna be enough. He had to pull out the extra artillery. That meant the elbow, which Kel proceeded to dig deep into Roger's back.

"Yeeeoowwww!" howled Kenan's dad. He leaned forward to try to escape the back rubbing torture that was coming from behind him. Kel leaned forward to keep up the pressure. He leaned a little too far; his feet slipped out from under him and he toppled over the chair, tackling Roger to the floor in the process. The two tumbled to the ground with a thud, Kel's fall broken by the fact that he landed on top of Mr. Rockmore's back, which made it a whole lot easier for him to keep up the massage. *Kenan's gonna be so proud of me,* he thought warmly to himself.

In the kitchen things weren't going a whole lot better. After searching the room for a cookbook, and only finding a book entitled *Cooking with Liver: 101 Tasty Liver Treats,* and since there was no way he was cooking liver, it looked like Kenan was on his own.

A quick search of the freezer turned up some

hamburger meat. Kenan's eyes perked up at that. *Hamburgers,* he thought. *How hard could those be to cook?*

That decision made, he pulled the frozen block of beef from the freezer and started to cook.

But the whole cooking thing seemed to be one problem after another. First, the meat was frozen together so solid that he wasn't able to break it up into individual hamburger patties. He tried breaking it in two, but that didn't work. Then he tried chipping at it with a knife, but the knife broke. He was just about to head to the garage for a saw, when an idea struck him. Why not just make one large hamburger and everyone could split it up later. That seemed like a fine idea.

Kenan rifled through the cabinets until he found a large cast-iron skillet. He hefted it up in his hands and dropped it onto the stove-top with a loud metallic clang.

A quick twist of the dial and the stove was on. He dropped the plastic-wrapped package of beef onto the skillet and stepped back to watch it cook. *This isn't so hard!* he thought to himself smugly.

"Get off of me!" Roger hollered, twisting his large frame back and forth violently in an attempt to dislodge Kel from his back.

"Not until you relax. All this tension is probably why your hair fell out," Kel responded as he pummeled Roger's back with his fists, up and down his spine.

"Somebody help me!" Roger begged, his voice trembling from the force of Kel's fists against his back.

This is gonna take forever. Kenan eyed the package of frozen beef that was sitting on the stove. A few tendrils of steam calmly drifted up from it, but the meat was still the same reddish-pink color it had been when he set it down about five minutes ago. It didn't seem to be cooking at all.

Kenan glanced around the kitchen, trying to figure out how to make it cook faster. His eyes scanned the appliances, searching for help. Blender, no help. Sink, no help. Cabinets, refrigerator, toaster: Hey! Maybe he could toast the meat. Nah, it would never fit into those little slots. *Let's see, Coffeemaker—no. Microwave— no—wait a minute! That's it!*

He grabbed the frozen block of beef and crammed it into the microwave. It barely fit, but Kenan managed to get the door closed.

"Five minutes oughtta do it," Kenan mumbled aloud as he punched in the numbers on the microwave's glowing digital display. *I'm sure it'll be fine,* he thought, and with a quick jab of his thumb onto the cook button, the microwave hummed to life.

For a few seconds everything seemed fine. The warm glow of the microwave lights bathed the plastic-wrapped hunk of beef in a bright yellow glow. The microwave hummed pleasantly to itself like it always did. The green glow of the numbers ticked off the seconds on the microwave's rectangular display. Everything was normal. Everything was like it always was. And then, everything turned bad.

First came the smell. A sharp whiff of ozone, like a match being struck, suddenly filled the air. Kenan's nostrils flared as they took in the smell. *Hmmm, I wonder what that could be?* he wondered.

His thought was answered a second later by a loud popping sound, which was followed by a bright flashing spark that flared to life inside the microwave. *Flash*

flash pop pop. The microwave flashed and shook like a fireworks celebration was being set off inside, like some kind of microwave version of the Fourth of July. Smoke began drifting up out of the top of the machine in thick gray belches.

Kenan's mouth dropped open in surprise as he gawked at the shower of sparks that was filling the inside of the microwave. It took a moment for him to take it all in. A moment before he was able to react. And then his whole body, all at once, leapt into action. He jumped up from the wooden kitchen chair he was sitting in and sprinted across the length of tile towards the exploding oven. He needed to stop it. To turn it off. But before he got there, the lights went out.

Everything in the kitchen was silent and dark. Not the normal kind of dark that you see at nighttime, which is partially lit by the warm glow of a clock, or the soft light of an outside lamp creeping in through the window. No, this was darker. And it wasn't just the kitchen, the whole house had gone black. The microwave slowed to a stop, seeming to sigh a sputtering, motory sigh of relief as it came to rest.

Sheryl stepped out of the bathtub just as the lights flickered and faded into blackness. "What the—" she murmured to herself as she ran her hand along the wall, groping for her robe. She found it and pulled it tightly around her slim figure. Next, she made her way to the nightstand where she always kept a flashlight. She clicked on the small plastic handheld lamp and headed downstairs.

As she approached the bottom of the staircase she heard the sounds of a struggle.

"Get off me!" Roger's deep bass voice pleaded.

"Not until you relax," came the mysterious reply from his shadowy attacker.

Sheryl swung the flashlight over towards the noise. Her brow furrowed, forehead creasing at the sight. It was Kel, sitting on her husband's back as he lay sprawled across the floor.

"Kel, get off of him. What are you doing?"

Kel stopped his massage and sheepishly climbed off of Mr. Rockmore. "He seemed a little tense, so I thought a back rub might be nice."

"Well what happened to all the lights?" she inquired in a way that did not at all sound happy.

Kel shrugged, drawing his shoulders up near his ears.

"Ummmmm," a new voice broke in, "I think that was my fault."

Sheryl swung the flashlight around, illuminating Kenan in its circular beam of light as he stood in the kitchen door like a deer caught in headlights.

"About dinner," Kenan continued, "I think we might want to order out."

Roger groaned as he pulled himself to his feet. "That does it, Kenan, you are grounded!"

"You can't ground Kenan," Kel protested.

"Oh yes I can," Roger roared. "And you, Kel, get out of my house."

"But . . . but . . ."

"OUT!!!" Roger extended one hand towards the door to point the way.

Kenan grabbed his friend and led him quickly towards the doorway. His dad didn't seem in any mood right now to deal with Kel. "I think you'd better go, Kel."

"Kenan," Kel groaned as they reached the exit, "I don't think they're gonna give us the tickets."

"I don't think so either," Kenan agreed. "But you know what, we'll just have to go to that game anyway and find another way in."

"But Kenan," Kel whispered to his friend, "if your parents are at the game, won't they see us?"

It was a good point, and Kel didn't make many good points. But Kenan wasn't going to let a little something like a good point get in the way of five thousand dollars. No, they were going to that game anyway. "We'll just have to go in disguise or something. Look, meet me back here tomorrow night. But you might want to come to my bedroom window so my parents won't see you."

"OUUUTTTT!" Roger bellowed.

"You better go. See you tomorrow." He shut the door after his friend, took a deep breath, and turned back around to face his parents.

"See, I can explain everything," he began, as his parents glared at him from across the room. He wiped his brow with one hand, and began trying to explain.

CHAPTER SIX

Grounded. Had his explanation meant nothing? Sure it was all a lie, but only because he knew that he couldn't tell his parents the truth about wanting the Bulls tickets. But just because it wasn't true was no reason for his parents not to buy it.

How could this have happened? It was supposed to be the best day of his whole life. Beating the McThunks, getting home just in time to watch two full hours of blood-sucking monkeys and, to top it all off, having fate hand him the announcement of the half-court contest that could win him and Kel five thousand dollars. Nothing was supposed to go wrong on a day like that. It was supposed to be a good day. A happy day. A day where all Kenan's plans worked out just right. But instead, here he was, a day later, the night of the Bulls game in fact, sitting in his room with no tickets. Plus, he was grounded.

Kenan lay flat on his back in his bed, which sat just underneath a wide-framed window that looked out, from its second-story view, across the Rockmores' backyard. The covers were pulled up tight around his neck as he stared up at the white, flat ceiling above him. He glanced over at the bedside clock, which stood on top of his dresser, just in front of a wall papered with posters and trading cards of sports heros and comic book superheros. The cold green numbers clicked over from 6:03 to 6:04 and then, as if just to taunt him, Kenan swore that the numbers switched back to 6:03 again. He closed his eyes and squeezed them tightly shut, then opened them again. The clock read 6:04. His mind was just playing tricks on him.

Thanks a lot, mind, he scolded his brain angrily, *I thought you were supposed to be on my side.*

A light rapping at his door caught his attention, and before he had the chance to answer, the door pushed its way open and his parents stepped in, looking somewhat less angry than they had the previous night.

"Hi honey, you doing okay?" his mother asked as she crossed the room and knelt by his bed.

Kenan let out an exaggeratedly sad and pathetic sigh, batting his large eyes up at his parents to complete the effect. "I'm fine," he said, not entirely convicingly.

Roger clapped his hands together. "Okay then, let's go to the game." He began rubbing his hands together a little impatiently.

"Roger," Sheryl scolded.

"What?" Roger answered defensively. "The boy's fine, now let's go to the game. Go Bulls!"

"Yeah, I'm fine." Kenan sighed sadly. "You two just go and have fun at the game." Kenan tried to force a smile, tugging his lips upwards until they formed a sort of half-smiling grimace. It was truly a pathetic sight.

Perfect, Kenan thought, *they don't suspect a thing.*

"Okay, well we're off to the game in a few minutes then. Your sister is staying over at a friend's, so you have the whole house to yourself."

Kenan looked dejectedly off into the corner of the room that he had selected as being the most pathetic. "Oh, that's okay. I'm just gonna lie here and stare at the ceiling and reflect on all the bad things I've done." He sighed once again just for effect, blinking his eyes sadly as he did.

"Okay then, let's go," Roger barked, motioning towards the door with a quick swing of his arms.

Sheryl stood and looked down at her son affectionately. Then she turned and headed for the door.

"Oh, Roger," Kenan heard her say as they walked down the hall. "I feel so bad for him. I think he's learned his lesson." And then their voices faded into the distance as they rounded the corner.

A bright smile appeared suddenly on Kenan's face from out of nowhere. They bought it! He yanked the covers off of his body, revealing that he was already fully dressed under the sheets. He even had his shoes on already. He was ready to put part two of his master plan into action. Part one, which had already worked so well, consisted of convincing his parents that he was so sorry about all the trouble he had caused. Part one had two benefits. First, if it worked well, and it had, his parents would probably un-ground him in the morning. And, second, they would never suspect that he was planning on sneaking out of his house, donning a disguise, and heading to the Bulls game with Kel. It was a good thing that they would never suspect that, since that was part two.

Tap tap. Tap tap tap. A soft rapping came from the window. *Perfect, Kel's right on time.* Kenan congratulated himself on the brilliance of his plan, then turned towards the window and jumped back in surprise.

Sitting on the ledge outside his window, just under the branches of the large oak tree that stood guard outside their house, was something strange and frightening.

Kenan let out a sharp yelp of surprise and clutched at his chest as he stared at the pale white, pasty face that was pressed against the glass. The ruby red lips of the thing outside the window seemed almost painted upwards into a creepy, oversized smile. And the bright green hair that stood straight up off its head was almost an eerie counterpoint to the bulbous red nose that protruded in a perfect circle from its face.

Kenan stopped and looked again. There was something about the face at the window. Something about the red nose and the green hair and the floppy shoes that seemed to ring a bell.

A clown! Which was followed almost immediately by the thought, *What's a clown doing outside my window?* Another even more bizarre thought rushed quickly into his brain on the heels of that one. *And why's a clown drinking orange soda?*

Kenan's eyes narrowed. There was something oddly familiar about that clown. He walked to the window and pulled it open.

"Hey, Kenan!" the clown said, his bright red lips widening into a loopy, gap-toothed clown smile.

Kenan's eyes widened as the realization struck him. "Kel!" he exclaimed as he dragged his friend through the window, sending him tumbling down on the bed, floppy shoes flailing in the air. "What are you doing in that ridiculous clown outfit?"

"It's my disguise!" he answered proudly as he

adjusted the red bulb that perched precariously on the tip of his nose.

Kenan took a step away from his bed and stared at his friend with a stunned look. Kenan never knew quite what to expect with Kel around. But this was even more unexpected than most of the unexpected things that Kel happened to do unexpectedly. Truth be told, though, it was also kind of funny. Kenan tried not to smile, but a grin fought its way onto his face just the same.

Kenan actually had good reason to smile. Kel did make a pretty ridiculous-looking clown. It wasn't just the fact that he was wearing clown makeup. It was also the fact that he had applied it so badly. Now that Kenan could get a good look at Kel's face under the bright bedroom lights, he realized that the white clown makeup didn't actually cover his whole face. It was applied in big white clumps, which were splotched across his face like paint that had been slung onto a canvas by a diseased rhinoceros with really poor eye-hoof coordination.

On top of the splotchy patches of white, a red clown smile had been drawn across Kel's lips. But he didn't seem able to get both sides of the smile even. As a result, the smile on the left side of the clown's face seemed ridiculously large, as the red lips stretched clear up to his eyebrows, while the right side seemed almost sad in comparison.

"Kel," Kenan snickered. "Man, when I said to wear a disguise, I didn't really mean disguise yourself as a clown. I was thinking more like a fake mustache or a pair of glasses or something."

Kel shoved his hands deep into his pockets. "Don't worry, Kenan, I got that covered." He pulled a hankie out of his pocket. But this was no ordinary hankie, ordinary hankies didn't stretch on forever and ever. The more he pulled, the more hankie came out of his pocket, each length of handkerchief a different brightly colored pattern. Blue checked squares, red polka dots, then plaid patterned cloth emerged from his pocket in one continuous hankie string.

"I know I've got it in here somewhere," Kel mumbled to himself as he pulled out foot after foot of hankie. Finally, he reached the end and discarded the twelve feet of hankie onto the floor and plunged his hand into his other pocket. "Ah-ha!" he announced grandly as he pulled a thick pair of plastic horn-rimmed glasses from his pants.

"Eh? Eh?" he commented proudly as he displayed the glasses in front of Kenan for his approval. "They're my dad's, I borrowed 'em for the night." He stuck the glasses onto his clown face, the thick Coke-bottle lenses distorting his eyes like two tiny fishbowls. His brown eyes, magnified through the lenses, looked like two gigantic clocks, far too large for the rest of his head.

"Can you even see in those?" Kenan asked. "I mean, your dad's practically blind."

"Sure I can see," Kel replied confidently as he stretched his arms out in front of himself like a sleepwalker and began stumbling across the room. "Over there you've got a . . . blurry thing. And right next to that is a big kinda blobby thing, and . . . on the wall over there is . . ."

SMASH! Kel walked straight into Kenan's dresser, sending the picture frames that were standing happily on top plunging to the ground.

"Hey, what's that noise?" Kel asked, startled. He stumbled back away from the noise, tripped over the endless hankie that lay on the floor, and tumbled forward into Kenan's desk, toppling his computer monitor off its stand with a loud crunch.

"Kel, would you watch what you're doing? You're making too much noise, my parents are gonna hear you." Kenan chased after his friend, trying to step in the way of Kel and further destruction.

"I'm sorry, I'll stop," Kel assured him before turning and walking straight into the wall. A large, nicely framed poster of Michael Jordan rattled off of its hook and dropped to the floor with a heavy thud.

"Would you—Shhhhh!" Kenan hissed at him.

Kel froze in place and pulled the glasses off his face. He winced apologetically towards his friend. "Sorry," he offered.

Kenan heard something. He leaned towards the door and listened closer. Uh-oh. Footsteps coming up the stairs.

"Uh-oh! Kel, my parents are coming. Quick, get back out the window!"

"But, Kenan, it's cold out there!"

But Kenan wasn't listening. He pushed his friend towards the open window and quickly shoved him out, dragging the window closed behind him just as the door to his room opened.

Kenan whirled around quickly and in one motion dropped the blinds in front of his window, obscuring Kel the clown behind a shield of plastic slats.

"Kenan, what is all that racket you're making up here?" Sheryl asked as she pushed her way into his room, followed immediately by her husband. They stopped as soon as they set foot through the door. Two mouths dropped open in unison as they took in the destruction and mess with one quick sweep of the eyes.

"What happened in here?" Roger boomed accusingly across the room at his son.

"Well . . . uh . . . see . . ." Kenan stalled for time. "Uh . . . what had happened . . . in here per se . . . was . . . uhm . . . See . . . I was just . . . uh . . ." finally he had it. "I was just testing the theory of gravity . . . you know, for school."

"What!" Both parents exclaimed it together.

Kenan was on a roll. He couldn't stop now. "Uh . . . yeah. See, watch." He plucked a small lamp from his dresser, held it out in front of him, and with a slight, barely perceptible wince, let it drop to the floor. The bulb shattered and sparked as the light flashed out. "Yep, it works, all right. Boy, that Isaac Newton, huh?"

His parents both stared at him in shock. Each one wondering silently why Kenan had to take so much after the other.

Roger spoke first. Ordinarily, he would have been upset, but then there was nothing ordinary about what he had just witnessed, and frankly, he wasn't quite sure how to react. "Would you just please not break anything else tonight? Please?" Both Kenan's parents stared at him with shocked, questioning expressions on their faces.

"Okay," Kenan agreed. "You got it Pop."

Sheryl nodded doubtfully. "Okay then. Well, we're leaving now for the game so . . . good night." She shot one last, curious glance towards her son, then with a shake of her head, the two of them stepped out of the room, pulling the door shut behind them.

Kenan collapsed on the bed and let out a huge sigh of relief. He dropped his head into his hands and marveled to himself at what a close call that had been. Then, he remembered Kel.

Quickly he yanked up the blinds. Kel was huddled into a shivering little ball of clown just on the other side of the glass. Kenan shoved the window open and reached a hand out to his oddly painted friend.

"Th-th-th-thanks," Kel stammered as he took his friend's hand and began to pull himself into the room.

The door to the bedroom cracked open again and Kenan quickly gave Kel a shove back out the window.

Unfortunately, he shoved a little harder than he intended to and Kel stumbled back over the windowsill and dropped off the edge of the roof, disappearing from view with a loud, surprised shriek.

"AHHHHHHHHHHHHHHHHHHHH!"

Kenan whipped around to see his parents standing, once again, in his doorway.

"Mom, Dad. Uh . . . hi." He tried hard not to sound guilty, but he didn't do a very good job of it.

"Kenan, what was that scream?" Sheryl asked, eyeing her son suspiciously.

"Scream?" Kenan asked innocently, as if he had no idea what his mother was talking about.

"Yes," his dad jumped in, rubbing one hand across his bald head in frustration. "That loud shrieking scream we heard when we walked in. What was it?"

Kenan's face lit up in recognition. "Oh, that scream. That was . . . me. I was just screaming because . . . it's such a . . . beautiful night out. Just makes you want to scream, doesn't it?"

Roger and Sheryl exchanged looks. "No," they both answered.

Kenan chewed nervously at half of his lower lip. "Oh, well, I guess it's just me then. Ahhhhhhhhh! Beautiful night," he screamed out the window to reinforce his story.

Before Kenan's parents could give any more attention to the thoughts that were running through their heads of hiring a mental health professional, they were interrupted by the shrill electronic beeping of the phone. Roger snatched the cordless off of Kenan's desk absently and jabbed at the talk button. "Rockmores," he answered sternly.

His deep-set eyes bugged out in concern as he listened at the phone. His large brow furrowed, three deep lines of worry creasing his smooth forehead.

"I see, thank you," he commented to the unknown voice on the other end of the line. Dropping the phone on the counter, he turned towards his wife.

"What is it, Roger?" Sheryl's voice wavered a little as she asked, preparing herself for bad news.

"It's Aunt Bertha. She ate some bad bologna again and now she's all puffed up like a blowfish." Roger held his thick hands out wide in a large circle to indicate the exact extent of the puffiness.

"Oh, not again," Sheryl moaned. It seemed that every other month, Aunt Bertha was being sent to the hospital from extra bloat. And the bologna was always the worst one. "We'd better go and see her. I guess we won't get to make the game after all."

Roger tipped his head from side to side like a child who has had his favorite toy taken away. "Awww, can't we go see her after the game? I'm sure she'll still be swollen."

Sheryl didn't answer. She didn't have to. All she did was raise one eyebrow ever so slightly. But it was enough.

"Oh, all right," Roger conceded. "Do you want to come Kenan?"

Kenan hadn't really been paying attention. He was too busy thinking about how amazing his luck was. His parents had two tickets to the Bulls game. Two tickets that they would no longer be using. *Boy, life is good sometimes,* Kenan marveled.

"Kenan!" his father repeated. "Do you want to come?"

Kenan jerked his head up, broken out of his own private reverie. "Oh," he answered, "you know, ordinarily I would love to go and visit Aunt Bertha at the hospital. But, you know, I'm feeling a little sick right now." He hacked out a couple of coughs to illustrate his point, then continued, "And I wouldn't want to get puffy old Aunt Bertha any sicker than she already is, so . . . I guess I'll just stay here."

"Fine," Sheryl answered as she and Roger headed for the door. Kenan quickly followed after them, stepping in between his parents as they padded softly down the hall towards the stairs. Without missing a beat, Kenan continued. "It's too bad though that you're gonna miss that Bulls game. You know, such a shame to see those tickets go to waste and all. By the way—" he began, as if the thought had just occurred to him. "Where are those tickets anyway?"

His parents weren't fooled in the least.

"Don't worry, Kenan. The tickets are safe from you," Roger explained. "They're not even here. They're waiting for us at the arena."

They reached the bottom of the stairs as Roger finished his sentence. He was too busy heading for the door to notice the huge smile that had suddenly leapt to life on Kenan's face. Kenan tried to fight the smile off, rubbing his hands over his mouth to hide his glee.

"Oh well, say hi to Aunt Bertha for me." He waved a hand in his parents' direction as they grabbed their coats, opened the door, and headed out.

Kenan stepped into the open doorway, shivering as the cool evening breeze washed over him, adding to the excited shivering that his body was already busily engaged in.

"Bye-bye." He waved as the car roared to life, headlights bathing Kenan in their blinding yellow glare.

Kenan sighed to himself as the car slowly crawled out of the driveway with a low purr. And then Kenan screamed!

The clown jumped out of the bush, twigs sticking out from its green hair at all angles. The once white face was now covered in thick patches of brown dirt like some kind of clown zombie that had been raised from the dead to entertain the children of the world.

Kenan staggered back, lost his balance, and dropped to the ground.

Kel spat a clump of dirt from his smudged and dirty red mouth. "Sheeesh. What's your problem?" he asked. Then he shrugged, stepped over his friend with one big floppy shoe, the other shoe somehow having escaped during Kel's plummet into the bushes, and with an odd, lumbering sort of half-floppy limp, stepped into the house to get cleaned up.

CHAPTER SEVEN

The arena rose up from the windy Chicago streets like a giant, domed spaceship. The immense concrete structure stretched for blocks in all directions. A huge saucer of mortar and stone that had been plunked down in an otherwise unassuming field of asphalt. A row of glass doors lined the outside wall in a large circle like some kind of reverse aquarium staring out onto the outside world.

A wide concrete pathway wound its way from the parking lot, up a short row of stairs that stretched the length of several large minivans across the front of the complex, and finally made its way up to the main entrance of the building.

Fountains spraying water high into the air turned various shades of red and green and blue and salmon as rows of colored spotlights flickered on and off from underneath the spray, bathing the water in their colored glow. And beyond the fountains, beyond the squat rectangular ticket hut that jutted out from the front entrance like a large angular nose sticking out from an otherwise round, concrete face, beyond the army of stantions that marked out a winding maze of a line, just above the gleaming glass of the front doors, was a huge banner that proudly proclaimed the reason for all of this. The banner read "Welcome to the home of the World-Famous Chicago Bulls." The red bullhead insignia was stamped bright and clear across the center of the sign like a guard dog with horns. There was an electric chill in the air around the building. This was a historic basketball monument.

If you listened closely you could almost hear the roar of fans from the past as they screamed to the slam-dunking heroics of their home team. The thrill of victory, the agony of defeat, and, of course, in the off-season, the magical joy of skaters dressed like mice on ice, hung ghostlike in the air around the arena, filling the atmosphere with an exciting, emotional charge.

Four thin wheels spun rapidly underneath their small metal frames, the spokes blurring together from the motion until they became one grayish cloud that hung dark and ominous between the tires as the two bicycles sped up to the arena. Kenan and Kel didn't really take in the majestic feel of the place. Nor did they feel any charge of emotion or excitement as they pulled their bikes to a stop in front of the building. What they felt was exhaustion.

Sweat ran down Kenan's face in a torrential downpour. His whole body seemed like some teenage version of a rain forest. His muscles ached. His lungs ached. Even his fingernails ached. He panted, sucking in air like a man that had been holding his breath for about twenty years and who had finally decided to breathe again.

"Man!" he gasped, his voice high and raspy. "Ten

miles didn't seem so far until we started pedaling." It took him a while to finish the sentence, since he had to gasp for air in between every syllable. "You okay, Kel?" He turned towards his friend on the bike next to him. Only there was no bike next to him. There was nothing next to him except the cool night air.

"Kel?" he asked as his eyes searched from side to side for his vanished friend. Finally he cast his gaze downward.

Kel lay flat on his back next to his overturned bicycle. His limp limbs were splayed out like a starfish that was pointing in all directions as he stared wide-eyed up into the nighttime sky. His freshly scrubbed face had been wiped clean of all clown makeup, but had now turned a sort of grayish color all its own.

"Ehhhhhhhhhhhhhhhhhhh!" he moaned loudly. Then, after a brief pause to catch his breath, he added, "Oohhhhhhhhhhhhhhhhhh!" His pale blue hat sat askew atop his head as if even it didn't have the energy to hold itself upright.

"Ahhhhhhhhhhhhhhhh!" Kel groaned as he panted for breath on the cold rough asphalt ground of the parking lot.

Kenan climbed slowly down from his bike, his shaking muscles screaming in protest with every move. He leaned the bike against a nearby tree and quickly wrapped his chain around it before kneeling down in front of his fallen friend.

"Kel, get up!"

"I can't."

"You have to. We've come this far. We can't stop now."

"But Kenan, I can't feel my legs," Kel whined.

Kenan grabbed Kel's knee and squeezed. "Feels fine.

Now let's go!" he ordered. "We've already missed the first period of the game. We're running out of time. Now get up."

Grabbing hold of his arms, Kenan yanked and tugged and pulled and prodded and pushed his weary friend to his feet.

"Hey, now I can feel my legs," Kel stated excitedly as he wobbled from side to side. "And they hurt!" he finished with a low screaming moan.

Kenan clutched his friend by the shoulders and jerked him around until they were face-to-face. He locked a steely eyed glare directly onto Kel's own, wavering gaze. "Look," he stated with authority, "I'm tired too. But that doesn't matter right now." His voice rose to a feverish rallying sort of pitch.

"All that matters," he continued, "is that we can win five thousand dollars for throwing a basketball into a net. And with that five thousand dollars we can buy all the orange soda that you can drink!" His voice rose proudly into the night air, hung for several dramatic moments, and then quietly faded away into the distance.

The speech worked. Kel's jaw set in determination. Kenan was right. Especially about that orange soda part. They could do it. "All right!" he shouted dramatically. "Let's go!"

Percy Higgins didn't exactly love her job. She worked the ticket booth at the Bulls Arena. That meant that it was her job to sell tickets and reserve tickets over the phone for people who would pick them up later, and it was her job to let the people in line who wanted tickets know when there were no more tickets to be had.

It wasn't really the ticket part of her job that Percy disliked. In fact, she was quite fond of the small, rectangular pieces of paper with their small concise lettering. What she really didn't like about her job were the people. People, in Percy's opinion, were overrated. Tickets, on the other hand, seemed to be rated just about right. You never heard tickets complain about the prices of things. Tickets never whined that their seats weren't good enough. Tickets never said, "Percy, you shouldn't sleep on the job," or "Percy, you can't be so rude to the people," or "Percy, what are you doing talking to those tickets? What are you? Some kind of weirdo?" No, tickets hardly ever said anything like that. People, on the other hand, seemed to say that kind of thing to Percy all the time.

She sighed and settled her plump frame back in the small, not-terribly-comfortable seat that was provided for her. She wiggled back and forth, shifting her weight from side to side as she struggled to find the least uncomfortable position for her rear end. Finally she settled in and, lifting a ticket to her face, she began to talk to it.

"Would it kill them to give me a comfortable chair? Would it?" she asked the small piece of paper. Her long brown hair was pulled back away from her face into a tight, straight ponytail, matching her lips, which were drawn back away from her cheeks in a tight, straight frown.

"What are you doing?"

Percy stared at the ticket and blinked. She turned it over in her hands, narrow eyes squinting up even narrower as she examined it. Had the ticket actually spoken to her? She pulled it close to her mouth and watched it carefully as she spoke.

"Are you talking to me?" she asked, enunciating each word loudly and clearly, like someone talking to a small child or a foreigner who might not understand English all that well.

"Nah, it's not the ticket talking. It's me. You know, right here . . . in front of you."

Percy glanced up from behind the ticket and frowned at the person standing in front of her. People were always wanting things from her. "Give me a ticket," or "How much is that ticket?" or "Are there any tickets left?" Want. Want. Want. And she was sure that this new person, with his friendly face and his friendly eyes and his even friendlier dreadlocks, was no different.

"What do you want?" she asked in a particularly unhelpful tone of voice.

"Uh . . . well, I think you have some tickets here for me. Rockmore's the name." Kenan slapped his hand down on the counter and began drumming his fingers impatiently as he waited for his tickets.

Percy didn't move quite so fast. First she glared at him for an extra second. Then, ever so slowly, she pulled herself out of the uncomfortable chair that she occupied and slowly dragged herself across the room to the computer. She extended one long pointer finger and began to jab at the keys one at a time. R . . . O . . . X . . . she wasn't much of a typist. Either that or she just didn't care. She deleted the X and continued. C . . . K . . .

Kenan's feet proceeded to perform a cement drumroll as they tapped rapidly against the pavement. *How long is it gonna take this woman to type Rockmore?*

"Hey!" Kel yelled off into the distance.

Kenan turned and cocked his head and watched curiously as Kel raised his hands high above his head and began waving them rapidly back and forth. It looked like he was trying to signal a flying saucer or a passing airplane, or maybe he was just trying to wave to somebody way back in the parking lot.

"Kel?" Kenan's voice rose to an inquisitive pitch. "What are you waving at?"

Kel threw a glance back in Kenan's direction. "Your parents," he said with perfect calm as he turned and resumed his waving.

"Oh." Kenan shrugged to himself. He turned back to the ticket window where Percy was still busily punching in letters on the computer. Suddenly, he froze, as a short, sharp, shriek leapt up from his belly and shot out of his mouth. His hands clenched up into tight fists and swung wildly at the air in front of him.

In one quick blur, Kenan spun and bolted over to Kel. "Kel?" he asked with a forced sense of calm. "What did you mean when you said that you were waving to my parents?"

Kel turned towards his friend. "Well, Kenan," he explained, "a wave is a form of greeting that's offered by the shaking of the—"

Kenan smacked him lightly on the chest. "Nah! I meant, why are you waving to my parents? They're at the hospital with Aunt Bertha."

Kel furrowed his brow. "No they're not. They're right there." He pointed off into the asphalt distance of the parking lot. Kenan screwed up his eyes as he stared at the people, small as dots across the long length of parking lot. He spotted a large, bald-headed dot who was walking next to a shorter, prettier dot. There was no mistaking who those dots were, even from far away.

"Awww, it's my parents!" Kenan squealed.

"Told ya."

"Awwww, maaaan!" Kenan looked around, pacing from one foot to the other with a caffeinated jitter. "We gotta do something. I'm supposed to be grounded. If they catch me here, they're gonna . . . ground me again."

His eyes grabbed on to a large, leafy bush that sat calmly just off to the side of the ticket booth. It didn't seem concerned at all about Kenan's encroaching punishment, but then, it was just a plant.

"Come on!" Kenan clutched a handful of Kel and yanked him into the bush, pulling the branches tightly in front of them as they watched Kenan's parents approach.

"I can't believe Aunt Bertha un-puffed so quickly!" Sheryl marveled to her husband as she strolled at his side, lovingly clutching his large hand in her own.

"I know!" Roger nodded along. "She deflated just like a balloon. Isn't modern medicine amazing?!"

The two of them stepped past a quietly unassuming little bush, which seemed to rustle nervously at the sight of them, and then, without even a glance in its bushy direction, they walked up to the ticket booth.

E . . . Percy punched the last letter of Rockmore into the computer with a pudgy jab of her finger. The printer hummed to life and began spitting out their tickets with a noisy, electronic chatter, like a small chipmunk had gotten loose in there and was now running wild.

With utter and amazing lack of speed, Percy slowly tore the tickets from the printer and shuffled back to the counter just as Roger and Sheryl stepped up.

"Rockmore. Here are your tickets." Her flat voice dripped with boredom as she handed the tickets across the counter to Roger and Sheryl. She didn't seem to realize that they weren't the same people who had asked for them earlier. Either that, or she just didn't care.

"Wow!" Sheryl exclaimed in genuine surprise. "You're the fastest ticket seller I've ever seen."

"I hear that a lot," Percy droned monotonously, then set about trying to adjust herself into her chair once again.

Kenan and Kel peered out through the curtain of branches and leaves that hid them from view. They watched as Kenan's parents took the tickets that had almost been theirs. They watched as Roger and Sheryl, tickets in hand, walked off. And they watched as the elder Rockmores headed towards the arena and . . . walked straight into a giant leaf!!! Oh, wait, no. That leaf was actually just in front of Kenan and Kel's faces. Roger and Sheryl actually walked straight into the arena, unobstructed by any large, green foliage.

"Man!" Kenan pushed his way out of the shrubbery, the branches protesting in a cacophony of rustles and snaps as he and Kel stepped from their hiding place. "Stupid Aunt Bertha," he mumbled to himself. "Having to get all better and stuff."

Kel tugged at his shoulder with both hands. "Kenan, what are we gonna do now? Your parents took our tickets!"

A thought began to gnaw at Kenan's gut. An unpleasant thought. A thought that said, "Give up! Go home! Your plan is not gonna work." The thought crawled its way up into Kenan's belly, which twisted and knotted and grumbled uncomfortably. "Oh, and by the way, I'm hungry!" the thought added as an afterthought.

Pressing the heel of his hand into his belly, Kenan

pushed the thought away. They couldn't give up yet. There had to be a way to get tickets to that game.

"Excuse me, ma'am. Remember me, from before?" He flashed his biggest, brightest, most memorable smile across the counter.

Percy Higgins glanced up, a pool of annoyance glazing her tiny eyes. "No," she muttered.

"Yeah, well, never mind about that. I was just wondering." Kenan made sure to keep his tone light and friendly as he asked, "Would there happen to be any more tickets for tonight's game?"

Two pairs of hopeful, expectant eyes stared across the counter at Percy as Kenan and Kel leaned in eagerly, awaiting her response.

Percy shifted her gaze back to the book that was propped open across her lap. "No," she retorted.

"Well, do you think that maybe you could just check again, just one more time, for us?" As Kenan asked the question, Kel offered up a big, broad, please-help-us kind of smile. He batted his eyes up at her like a lost puppy dog.

Unfortunately, Percy hated puppy dogs. "No." She didn't even bother looking up at them this time.

"Yeah, but—"

"No." She interrupted him, rudely signaling that the conversation was over.

Kenan stomped his foot loudly against the pavement. "Awww, man!" With an air of dejection floating around his hung head, he and Kel turned to leave. The tread on their shoes scuffed loudly across the pavement, their feet shuffling against the white cement as they went. Suddenly a voice rang out from behind them. It was Percy's voice, but something was different about it. It sounded excited.

"Wait! I've found some tickets! Two tickets, right here."

Kenan bolted back to the booth.

"Really?!" he asked, panting from excitement.

Percy's gaze met Kenan's and held it as a small hint of a smile pried its way onto her face.

"No," she said. "Heh, heh. Just kidding."

Kenan grumbled as he made his way back to Kel.

"Well," Kel said, "I guess we should go back home now. Huh, Kenan?"

But Kenan wasn't watching him. Wasn't paying attention to what he was saying. Kenan's mind was somewhere else. A faraway scheming kind of glint gleamed in his large brown eyes as he snapped his head in his friend's direction.

"Oh, the only place we're going is inside that arena!" he boomed into the night.

One corner of Kel's lip began involuntarily to tremble. It was what always happened when Kenan was scheming. "How?" he asked nervously.

"That," Kenan said, "is a very good question."

CHAPTER EIGHT

He shoots! He scores! Two points for the Bulls. Boy the Orlando Magic are taking a pounding tonight at the hands of this powerful Chicago team." The announcer's voice crackled over the tiny speaker with static-laced enthusiasm.

Bob, the security guard, smiled and pumped his fist in the air as the cheering of the crowds inside the arena roared out to the front doors where he stood.

He held the tiny, frog-sized radio closer to his ear so that he could hear the announcer over the roar of the crowd inside. Something caught his eye. Some movement. Footsteps were approaching him quickly. He glanced up from the stool where he was leaning and saw two boys trying to walk past him and into the arena.

"Whoa, whoa, whoa there," he said, his thick voice dripped with a Southern accent that added a slow twang to his speech.

"Just where do you think you're going?" He pushed

himself off the stool and sauntered slowly over to the two boys.

"Well," the one with dreadlocks answered in an innocent-sounding voice. "We were just gonna go in and catch the game."

The security guard hooked his thumbs up under his belt. "Well that's certainly no problem, if you've got a ticket. Do you have tickets?" he asked.

The skinnier one with the hat jumped in quickly to answer, "No!"

"No . . . no . . ." The other one was talking now. The security guard kept swinging his head from one to the other like a spectator in some kind of really demented tennis match. "No . . ." he continued. "No tickets . . . on us. See, what had happened was"—he stepped in close to Bob and lowered his voice as if he were passing on confidential information—"see, my parents have our tickets, but we were running a little late and so they went in without us. See?"

"Nah, Kenan," his friend chimed in, "that's not what happened. See, what happened was—"

"Kel!" Kenan seethed. "That is too what happened."

Kel shook his head from side to side, his blue hat swaying slightly as it perched on his head. "No it isn't."

Kenan slowly turned to glare at his friend. "Yes," he hissed through clenched teeth, "it is."

"No," Kel replied slowly and helpfully, "it—"

SMACK. A quick hand lashed out and knocked Kel on the back of the head. His hat tipped down over his face and then dropped to the floor. Kel quickly retrieved it and, rubbing his head gingerly with one hand, he finally added, "Yes it is."

Kenan turned and flashed a bright smile towards the security guard. "See. That's what happened. So, can we go in?"

Bob looked at the both of them for just a moment before replying with a bemused smirk, "No. I'm sorry, but I just don't believe your story."

"Really?!" Kel stepped up to him as he asked with surprise, "Which part?"

Two surgeons rushed up to the front door of the arena. They had important surgeon business to attend to. Their white surgeon coats flapped behind them in the wind. Their green surgeon masks busily hid their boyish not-so-surgeon-like faces. A small dreadlock peeked out from underneath one of the green, shower-cap hoods. And the other hood seemed to be pulled tightly over a bright blue hat.

Bob eyed the two surgeons suspiciously as they rushed their way up to the front, barking surgeon orders at no one in particular.

"Can I help you two?" he asked.

"Yes!" the first surgeon barked as he quickly tucked the rogue dreadlock back underneath the hood. "We must get inside. One of the players is injured and needs to be operated on immediately!" He began pushing his way towards the glass front door. A hand shot out, blocking his path.

"Well, that is interesting. Which player is it?" Bob asked skeptically.

"Uh . . . it's . . . uh . . ."

The second surgeon jumped in quickly, "It's the one with the legs."

"Yes," the first surgeon continued, not seeming very

happy with his partner's answer. "The one with the legs." The dreadlocked surgeon seemed to glare out at his hat-wearing colleague from underneath the green surgical mask he wore.

"Oh, I see." Bob rocked back on his heels and crossed his arms in front of his chest. "What's wrong with him?" He eyed the two surgeons carefully as they desperately fought to make up an answer.

"It's his . . . back. Yes, his back. We have to perform an emergency spine . . . ectomy or else he'll never . . . uh . . ." he faltered.

"He'll never sing again!" the other surgeon leapt to the not-quite-a-rescue.

A beefy security guard hand reached out and plucked the mask away from the closer surgeon's face.

Kenan winced, scrunching his face up guiltily as Bob glared at him. "Ohhhhhhh!"

"Pizza! We got a pizza delivery for the Chicago Bulls. Right here, pizza for the Bulls! Excuse me, sir!"

Bob glanced up at the two pizza delivery boys that stood in front of him holding a large pizza box in each hand.

"Yeah?" he asked as he stayed firmly planted on his stool.

"We got a pizza for the Bulls. They just called in and ordered it. They wanted it here by halftime so, we're just gonna rush on in and deliver it. So, if you could just hold the door for us, then . . ."

Bob stood, but instead of going to open the door, he opened up one of the pizza boxes.

"This is empty."

"Well that's . . . because . . . uh . . . they ordered

it . . . plain? Ohhhhhhh!" Four empty pizza boxes crashed to the ground as Kenan and Kel once again were marched away.

"Man, it's almost halftime," Kenan complained as he paced back and forth in front of his friend. "We're never gonna get in."

Kel shot a single finger up in the air. "I've got it!" he announced proudly. "We can dress up as cheerleaders!"

Kenan's mouth hung agape as he shot a bewildered look at Kel. "That's never gonna get us inside!"

"Oh, I know. I just thought it would be fun to dress up as cheerleaders."

Kenan started to say something and then stopped. He had absolutely no idea how to respond to that. He finally decided to respond by sinking to the ground, clutching his head in his hands and moaning, "Oh, this is hopeless."

Kel plopped himself down on the concrete beside his friend. "I know," he agreed. "If only there was a back door or something."

Kenan's head shot up out of his hands.

The back of the arena looked a lot like the front, except that there were fewer doors, no ticket booth, no fountains, and no wide sidewalk leading the way to the entrance. Actually, it looked nothing like the front.

An extremely large man, who looked as though he could have easily been a professional wrestler if only he were a little less mean, stood in front of the single rear door to the arena. His arms, which seemed like someone had blown up balloons really big and then stuffed them under his skin, were folded neatly in front of his black shirt, resting just above the white stenciled letters that spelled out the word "security" across his swollen and bulging chest.

Kenan and Kel peered at him from around the corner. He looked mean, he looked tough, thankfully, though, he didn't look all that bright.

"Kenan, he looks all mean and tough!" Kel clutched tightly on to Kenan's arm, a look of fear and worry etched across his narrow features.

"Don't worry, Kel." Kenan smiled confidently. "I got a plan!"

The burly back-door security guard glared angrily out from underneath his muscular forehead. Even his eyebrows seemed to be in better shape than the eyebrows of most people. They definitely weren't eyebrows you would want to run into in a dark alley. Partially because they were pretty tough-looking as far as eyebrows went. Mostly, though, you wouldn't want to run into them because they happened to be attached to the rest of the security guard.

Two other security guards who looked far less intimidating in their black security T-shirts, sauntered up to the back door.

"Some night, huh?" the first of the new security guards said as he ran his hands through his stubby dreadlocks.

A pair of muscular eyebrows shifted position to glare at the two newcomers. Large nostrils flared. "Who are you two?" The voice was a deep, rumbling growl, almost like the roar of a really intimidating lion.

Kenan and Kel gulped simultaneously. Kenan tried

to speak again, but all the saliva seemed to have suddenly fled his throat and all he managed was a dry, cracked, squeaky sound.

"What?!" the guard snarled.

Kenan fought hard to recover his voice and continue. "Uh . . ." he began nervously. "Uh . . . see, we're your replacements. Yeah, uh . . . you know, so you can take a break and we'll guard the door for you until you get back."

The guard's large brow creased from the strain as he tried to think. "Really?"

Kel swallowed hard. "Yeah," he added meekly.

Both boys waited, trying to fight back the fearful trembling that had gripped all of their limbs and muscles and organs.

"Okay, great, thanks!" The guard offered up something vaguely resembling an overly muscled smile. Then he turned to leave, slapping Kel thankfully on the back. Kel dropped to the ground like a sack of potatoes that was dropped from a very high flying airplane.

"Uh . . . sorry," the guard offered with a burly shrug.

"Oh, no, no. Don't worry about it," Kenan protested. "He's fine. He just . . . tripped or something, that's all. Enjoy your break." Kenan waved good-bye as the security guard lumbered off around the corner.

"Kenan!" Kel moaned. "I think he broke me."

Kenan knelt next to his friend and helped him to his feet. "No he didn't, Kel. You're fine. Now come on." And with that, he turned and rushed into the arena.

A moment later, Kenan pushed the door open and popped back outside. Kel was still there, standing with his arms folded in front of him.

"Kel?" he inquired politely. "What are you doing out here still?"

Kel looked at his friend as if he were stupid. "I'm guarding the door until that guy is done with his break. Just like we were hired to do. Sheeesh!"

"Would you get in here!" Kenan snatched Kel tightly by the wrist and yanked him through the door. They were in.

Kenan and Kel found themselves in the long circular lobby, which wrapped itself around the outside of the arena court and seats like a scarf around a really thick neck. The whole area was taken up with concession stands selling food and drinks, souvenir stands selling Bulls T-shirts and Bulls basketballs and Bulls underwear and even Bulls toothpaste. Wide-open arches at regular intervals led out of the lobby and deeper into the arena where the court and the seats were. And from the arches loud screams and cheers interrupted the otherwise calm silence. A few random people wandered here and there around the lobby, but for the most part, except for vendors, it was pretty deserted. Everyone was in their seat, glued to the game as it raged on towards halftime.

"Okay, Kel, we did it, we're in!" Kenan practically patted himself on the back in congratulations.

"I just have one question, Kenan. Where did you get these security T-shirts from anyway?"

A shifty-eyed look danced its way across Kenan's face. "Heh-heh. Heh. Heh-heh-heh." He laughed to himself. "I can't tell you that. It's a secret!" he stated before resuming more of his private laughter. "Now come on, let's get to work."

Kenan and Kel started to move. Started to put the rest of Kenan's plan into action. But suddenly, Kel stopped. Something had caught his attention. A voice. But it wasn't the tone of the voice that made Kel stop and freeze. It was something that the voice was saying. Something important. Something amazing. Something fruit-flavored.

"Get your orange soda here!" the voice yelled.

Kel's eyes opened wide. Then they opened even wider. His mouth hung open and all of his taste buds began pleading with his brain.

"Kenan," Kel said in an awed half whisper. "That man is selling orange soda."

Kenan shot his friend an annoyed glance. "So?"

"So? I love orange soda!!" Kel screamed his orange love to the rooftop before turning and racing off after the magical sound of the voice. "Orange soda, I'm coming for you."

"Kel, with the—But the—'Cause it's—Awwwww!" And suddenly, Kenan was alone.

"Hi. How much for a cup of orange soda?" Kel hopped up and down in excitement imagining the beautiful orange soda spilling into a large cup that was meant only for his lips.

The weathered old man behind the counter eyed Kel up and down before answering. "Well, Security drinks free," he stated.

Kel threw his arms down against his sides. "Awww, man," he complained, "I wish I was Security."

The wrinkles in the old man's face deepened ever so slightly as he cocked his elderly head slightly to one side. "But, you are Security." He scratched at his light gray beard with one aged hand.

"What are you talking about?"

"Well," the gravely old voice grated, "you're wearing a Security shirt. So, doesn't that make you Security?"

Kel stole a glance down at his own shirt. The old man was right. He was wearing a Security shirt. "Nah, you see this shirt was only so Kenan and me could sneak—" he started to explain but then stopped himself as a thought occurred to him.

"Security drinks free, huh?"

"Of course."

Kel thought hard. He scratched his chin thoughtfully. He gazed thoughtfully off into the distance. Finally, he figured it out.

"And I'm wearing a Security shirt. So I must be Security."

"Aren't you?" The old man seemed a little confused by the entire conversation. *Young people,* he thought, *are very confusing.*

"Well then," Kel continued excitedly, "I'll have twenty orange sodas!"

Kenan rushed up to the concession stand just a minute or so later. A pile of discarded cups littered the counter, each one bearing the evidence of a watery orange residue. The cups weren't just all over the counter, they had also begun to spill off the counter and pile up in clusters all over the floor.

A clearly frazzled old man stood behind the counter gesticulating wildly in Kel's direction.

"I've got no more orange soda!" he screamed, his weathered old hands jerking up and down to illustrate his point. "You just drank twenty cups' worth. That's all the orange soda I had."

Kenan screeched to a halt, slipped on one of Kel's

used cups, and skidded to a slamming halt against the side of the counter. "Ow!"

Kel looked over at Kenan and smiled broadly, his teeth glinting an odd tint of orange underneath the fluorescent lights. "Hey, Kenan! What's up?"

Kenan gradually peeled himself off of the counter. "What are you doing?" he demanded.

"Drinking orange soda! Security drinks for free."

The words hadn't even left Kel's mouth when suddenly he felt two hands grab him firmly by his head. Kenan had the exact same thing happen to him as two meaty palms pressed down against the sides of his face. The two of them were forcefully spun around to come face-to-face with the owners of the hands.

"McThunks!" Kenan whispered as an all too familiar pumpkin-sized head lolled right in front of him.

Next to him Brian's jagged smile stretched over his yellow teeth as he glared into Kel's face.

"Are these guys bothering you, Uncle Freddie?" Brian asked the weathered old man behind the counter.

Uncle Freddie! Kenan thought. Who knew the McThunks actually had a family. He had always secretly suspected that they were created in a laboratory somewhere. It would have explained a lot.

Uncle Freddie made his way around the counter to where his two nefarious nephews stood only inches away from Kenan and Kel. He jabbed a finger in Kel's direction and spoke angrily, "This one here. He drank all my orange soda and I didn't get to charge him because he's Security." He punctuated the last thought with another sharp jab of his finger in Kel's direction.

Pumpkin Head laughed. His gigantic planet-sized cranium shook wildly up and down as he spewed out a torrent of nasal sounding "Ha's." His brother filled in the reason for the laughter. "Security?" Brian spat. "These two? You gotta be kidding, they're not Security."

Kenan's face contorted up into several varying expressions of "Uh-oh" all at once. His brow furrowed, his eyebrows arched, his mouth dropped.

Several large and angry-looking veins bulged their way threateningly out of Uncle Freddie's forehead. "What!" he screamed, his gravely voice echoing angrily across the cement walls of the lobby.

It was time to go. Things weren't going very well for Kenan or his friend and he was fairly certain that sticking around the McThunks wasn't going to make the day get any better. He needed a distraction. But what?

"Look!" Kenan pointed eagerly off into the distance, past Billy's gargantuan noggin. "It's a guy selling really big hats!"

Billy's head jerked around to look. He'd been searching his whole big-headed life for a hat that would fit over his thick skull. As the large bulbous melon on his neck swung to the side, it pulled the rest of Billy's body off balance. His head lolled to the left and, like an anchor, it dragged the rest of his body down with it. Off balance, he toppled to the left, crashing into his brother and pinning him to the ground.

"Run!" Kenan yelled as he pushed himself away from the concession stand and took off in a furious sprint across the lobby. Kel quickly followed suit, rushing off after Kenan.

Uncle Freddie lunged after Kel, tripped over his pile of nephews, and fell to the ground on top of the heap of McThunks. By the time they all untangled their limbs and scrambled back to their feet, Kenan and Kel were gone.

The McThunks finished searching the bathroom, making sure to kneel down and press their faces to the floor in order to peer under each of the ten stalls that lined the wall.

"They're not here," Billy said dejectedly as the others helped him haul his larger-than-it-should-be head off of the bathroom floor. When one last searching glance around revealed nothing, the three of them turned and trudged on to continue their search.

Under the door of the last stall in the row, two pairs of feet dropped to the ground from off of the toilet where they were standing to avoid detection. The metal door of the stall pushed open slightly and two pairs of eyes peered through the crack. The door felt cold and clammy against their skin as their eyes darted back and forth to make sure the coast was clear.

"I think they're gone," Kenan whispered. He pushed the door open and they both cringed back against the porcelain toilet just in case. The door clanged against the metal wall beside it. The bathroom was still and silent. Relieved grins broke out across both faces as Kenan and Kel stepped out of their stall hideout and made their way quickly across the bathroom.

"Now come on, Kel, we have to go figure out a way to get you onto that court."

Suddenly, Kel stopped. "I can't go, Kenan."

"What is it?" Kenan asked with nervous quickness. "Do you see the McThunks?"

"No."

"Then what is it?"

"Remember those twenty cups of orange soda I drank?"

Kenan nodded along impatiently, waiting for the explanation.

"Well . . . I gotta go to the bathroom!!"

Kenan looked around, holding his hands out to gesture around the room to his friend. "Kel, this is the bathroom. We're in the bathroom."

Kel drew a hand across his forehead and sighed with relief. "Whew. That's good, 'cuz I really, really gotta go!"

"Thank you for sharing that, Kel. Now would you just go."

Beep! A loud electronic bleep blared its way over the loudspeakers that were mounted above the bathroom's door. An announcer's voice broke through and Kenan and Kel both craned their heads to hear what he was going to say. "Well, that sound means it's halftime," the deep, controlled voice explained.

"Ap!" Kenan let out a little squeal of panic. "Halftime! Kel, do you know what that means?"

Kel took a moment and thought about it. It wasn't coming to him right away, but he was sure that if he thought about it long enough, he would figure something out.

"That means that it's time for the half-court contest. We have to get you out there. Come on," Kenan said urgently.

Kel shifted uncomfortably from one foot to the other. His hand clenched the bottom of his shirt and tugged on it. "I can't, Kenan, I haven't gone to the bathroom yet."

Kenan started to tell him to go, but before he got the chance a stampede of people poured into the little bathroom like a herd of wild wildebeests on the rampage. The flood of onrushers stormed their way past Kenan and Kel and quickly pushed and shoved their way to the toilets. The halftime bathroom rush was on.

Kenan looked towards the doorway and saw a very familiar bald head poking several inches above the multitude of bathroom-goers. Kenan knew exactly what that meant. Trouble.

"AAAHHHHH!" he screeched in a short, high-pitched squeal. With one hand, he grabbed Kel by the shirt and pulled him into the nearest stall, slamming the door behind them.

"Kenan, what are you doing!" Kel pulled Kenan's hand off of his shirt and tried to wipe away the wrinkles that he had caused.

"My dad! My dad's out there."

Kel didn't seem to get it. "You're dad's out where?"

A look of frustrated impatience crossed Kenan's mouth as he cracked the stall door and shoved Kel's head towards it so that he could see.

"Ohhhhhh!" Kel ducked back into the stall and pulled the door firmly shut behind him. "What is your daddy doing out there?" Kel wondered with a shake of his head.

"He's going to the bathroom!" Kenan replied through clenched teeth.

Kel's face lit up as everything suddenly became clear in his brain. "Ohhhhh. That reminds me, Kenan"—his face scrunched up into a pathetic, uncomfortable look—"I gotta go to the bathroom, too!"

Kenan jerked his head in the direction of the white porcelain toilet that sat in between them. "Then go," he suggested firmly.

"I can't go with you in here!" Kel complained as he

pressed his legs together tightly and jumped up and down.

"Well I can't go out there!" Kenan exclaimed.

The speakers crackled to life with an electronic hum and the announcer's voice broke over it again.

"It's that time, sports fans. We're going to call out five sets of seat numbers. If you're sitting in one of those seats . . ." The announcer paused just slightly for dramatic effect. It worked. Everyone had stopped what they were doing and every head hung on to every single word that boomed forth from the speaker. ". . . then you get to join us at half-court and try your luck at a shot that's worth five thousand dollars."

A hush fell over the already hushed crowd as everyone scrambled to pull out their ticket stubs and wait for their number to be called.

"Seat 42B!" the voice announced dramatically. "Seat 20F. Seat 82Q. Seat—"

The announcer continued to call numbers, but a new sound drowned him out. It was a very familiar bass voice that erupted from a very familiar bald head.

"That's me!" Roger shrieked to the gathered crowds. "I'm seat 82Q! That's my ticket!"

A sharp elbow nudged its way into Kenan's ribs. "Hey, Kenan, your dad's gonna be out there with me when I make my shot. Isn't that cool?"

Kenan's face would have looked happy, if he were standing on his head. While standing on his feet, it just looked like a great big frown. "No, that's not cool." He grabbed Kel's elbow in one hand to prevent any further nudging of any further ribs. "If my dad is out there and you are out there . . . then we are busted!"

Kel's face dropped. "Oh, yeah. What are we gonna do?"

But Kenan wasn't listening. He was already thinking of a plan to get them on the court. He sat down on the toilet to think some more, but the toilet lid was still wide open and his butt dropped into the water with a cold, wet splash.

"Whhhyyyy?"

CHAPTER NINE

"**R**oger Rockmore! Phone call for Roger Rockmore!" A bright shock of red hair rose from the young man's head like some form of sunburned palm tree, or maybe a hair antenna. His almond-shaped eyes scanned the crowds, peering out from his young, lightly freckled face.

"Roger Rockmore?!" he screamed again to the crowd, then paused as he scanned the faces for a response.

"Man, no one is answering," he said as he turned to a nearby trash can.

Kenan's round face poked out from behind the trash can. His eyes expertly surveyed the crowd to make sure he was safe. Then, when he was certain, he emerged from hiding.

"Look, just keep yelling. He's gotta be around here somewhere." He patted the kid on the back, offered a quick "good job," then began to crouch back behind the trash can.

"I think I've had about enough." The kid turned to Kenan. "You can keep the twenty bucks. I'm just—"

Kenan was on his feet in a flash. His eyes fixed on a point off in the distance. Somewhere in the middle of the teeming mass of Bulls fans, Kenan had spotted something. "That's him," he said to himself and then turned and repeated it louder for his redheaded acquaintance. "That's him, right there. The big bald guy. You see him?"

The kid nodded. He saw him. Roger was a pretty hard guy to miss. "Now remember, you have to get him to come over to this broom closet." Kenan indicated a wooden door behind him with a slight shrug of his elbow. "And you gotta get the ticket, or else the deal's off."

"All right." The kid bobbed his head up and down in agreement. *What the heck,* he thought. *This seems like an easy way to earn twenty bucks.*

"Kenan, I really gotta go to the bathroom," Kel's voice called from behind another trash can.

"Hold it!" Kenan barked. "You can go soon."

The trash can seemed to groan in response. Kenan pointed his employee towards his dad and quickly hid himself behind his own garbage recepticle to watch what happened. The moist, pungent odor of garbage assaulted his nose as soon as he got back into position. *Man,* he thought, *why did I have to pick the stinky trash can?*

"Roger Rockmore! Phone call for Roger Rockmore!"

Roger reached out and clamped a huge hand over the kid's much smaller shoulder.

"I'm Roger Rockmore," he announced.

"Uh . . . there's a phone call for you. It's your son. If you'll just follow me." The kid turned and started back towards Kenan, but Roger still gripped his shoulder firmly, and Roger wasn't going anywhere.

"Take a message," he instructed, "I've got five thousand dollars to win." His voice rose to a ridiculously high and excited pitch as he pressed the winning ticket to his lips and kissed it.

Why couldn't this just be easy? the kid wondered. But he had come this far and, after all, it was twenty bucks.

"You uh . . . have to take it, sir." He was improvising now. He didn't know exactly what he was going to say next. He tugged nervously at the strands of hair that jutted up away from his skull as he continued. "Because . . . uh . . . it's an . . . emergency."

A look of parental concern flashed across Roger's face. "What is it? Is everything okay?"

"Uhm . . . no! No, it's not okay." The kid had a thought. "It has to do with . . ." He struggled to think.

"Your television," whispered Kenan from behind his trash can.

"Your television," the kid said quickly.

A thick hand shot to Roger's chest and he clutched at his heart in its meaty grasp. *No! It couldn't be,* he worried. *Not the TV! Anything but that!*

"Show me to your phone!" Roger's voice was weak and shaky. He felt his legs threaten to give out. He knew that, as a parent, someday he might have to face a moment like this one, but he had never expected it to happen so soon. He had to be strong.

The kid smiled to himself as he led Roger away across the crowded lobby.

"The phone is right through that doorway." The kid jabbed one pasty, freckled finger towards the broom closet.

Roger nervously grabbed the door and began to pull it open.

"Oh," the kid quickly added. "Before you use the phone, I'll need to see your ticket. You know, to verify your ID?"

Roger's mind was elsewhere. He wasn't really thinking about how odd a request that was. He wasn't really concentrating on how his ticket would verify his ID. He just quickly yanked it out of his pocket, flicked away several pieces of dry, gray lint, and passed the ticket over.

The moment the ticket was safely in the kid's hand, Kenan bolted from his hiding place and gave his dad a quick shove towards the door. Roger was caught off-guard. He didn't know what hit him. He tripped, stumbled backwards, and crashed through the doorway, landing on the floor of the broom closet. Before he even had time to realize what had happened, or who had done it, Kenan grabbed the door and pushed it shut. With a screeching grate of metal against tile, he dragged the garbage can over and stacked it in front of the door, just under the rectangular handle. With Kel's help, they moved a second trash can and stacked it on top of the first, sealing up the room in a barricade of garbage.

Whipping a twenty-dollar bill from his wallet, he quickly exchanged it for his dad's ticket. And, with a swift but meaningful "thank you," tossed in the direction of the redheaded kid, Kenan and Kel were off.

Kenan stuffed the ticket into Kel's open hand. "All

right, now get out there on that court and win us five thousand dollars."

Kel's whole body tensed up uncomfortably. "But I really, really, really have to go to the bathroom!" he moaned unpleasantly.

"Later!" Kenan snapped. "Right now, we gotta—"

"There they are!!" Billy McThunk's voice was unmistakable in its nasal wail as it boomed out across the lobby.

"Ahhhh! Run for it, Kel."

Kenan and Kel bolted off in separate directions, splitting their pursuers into two separate groups. Billy and Uncle Freddie raced off after Kenan, leaving Brian and his jagged smile to rush off after Kel.

Kel slipped through one of the wide-open arches that led to courtside. He decended a flight of stairs, leaping down the concrete steps two, sometimes three at a time. He could hear Billy's hot, mean breath panting into the air not far behind him.

Kel leapt to the bottom of the stairs, hopped a small wall, and dashed through a crowd of seated spectators as he rushed his way towards the court.

A loud crashing sound came from behind him and he guessed, correctly, that Brian hadn't quite hopped over the wall as neatly and easily as he had.

But those McThunks were nothing if not quick, and Brian was back on his feet in a flash and back on Kel's tail.

"I'm sorry, I'll need to see your ticket. Only the five people that were picked get to go on the court right now," the attendant said, stopping Kel at the edge of the court.

Brian was just behind him. Not far now. He pumped his bully legs faster, desperate to reach Kel.

Kel opened his fist and flashed the ticket that Kenan had stuffed there.

A quick glance and Kel was being waved through, just as Brian raced up from behind.

"I'm sorry, I'll need to see your ticket." The attendant stepped in front of Brian, stopping him as Kel jaunted his way down to the court.

The air vibrated as the voice of the announcer, all smooth excitement and slick control, flooded the speakers. "All right, all of our contestants have made it to the floor."

Kel stepped up in line next to the other four competitors. He hopped up and down, biting at his lower lip. His bladder inflated in pain. All he had to do was hold it in for a few more minutes and then it would all be over. That couldn't be that hard, just a few more minutes.

"Before we get started, let's not forget that tonight's half-court contest is brought to you by Gushing Fountains Bottled Water."

At the first mention of the word "gushing," Kel hunched over, clutching desperately at his side. The word "fountains" sent his insides into a fit. "Bottled," didn't really affect him that much, but when the announcer got to the word "water" . . . Kel had to go!

"That's right," the announcer continued. "If you want to pour yourself a nice cool glass of water, then you should drink Gushing Fountains Bottled Water."

Kel was in agony! He crumpled to the floor and began trembling. *Almost over. Almost over. Almost over.* He repeated it over and over again in his head. *Desert . . . Dry.* He tried hard to think of anything but water. *Orange soda—No! That was no good. Sand, sand, gushing sand, AHHHHHH!*

"Now let's welcome our first contestant . . ." Kel looked up, desperately hoping that he could be first so that he could get it all over with. "Elizabeth Leslie."

The short, middle-aged woman took center court and was handed a ball.

Kel began to cry.

Kenan darted around a corner, a pair of McThunks hot on his tail. He craned his head back over his shoulder to see just how close they were. They were close.

A short, sharp squeal escaped his lips and he tried to pick up his pace when . . . CRASH. Before he turned his head back around, he barreled into someone and the two of them crashed to the floor in a tangled pile.

"Oh, I'm sorry! I'm really—"

"Kenan?!" Sheryl pulled herself to her feet and stared down at her son in surprise.

"M-m-mom?" Kenan uttered from his spot on the floor.

She cocked one hand on her hip in a very motherly I'm-disappointed-in-you sort of way. "You had better have a good explanation for what you're doing here, young man."

Kenan swallowed hard. "Oh, I do. See, I . . . I . . . I . . . Ohhhhhh, I'm busted!"

Kel's insides were drowning. All of his internal organs were shouting for relief while trying to bail. He couldn't hold it much longer. Heck, he couldn't hold it any longer. But maybe, just maybe, he wouldn't have to. It was his turn. The ref placed a ball in his trembling hands and he stepped to center court.

* * *

Clang! Bam! Thud! Clang! The door to the broom closet budged open inch by inch, until finally, with one last shove, the garbage cans that were stacked in front of it tumbled to the floor and the door flew open. Roger was free. *Still time to win my five thousand dollars,* he thought as he sprinted towards the court.

Kel held the ball in his hand, waiting for the ref's whistle to let him know that it was okay to throw. The announcer kept up the tension.

"Well, this is our last contestant of the night. So far, no one has even come close to making it. But before we see this last half-court shot, let's pause and see a brief spot from our sponsors, Gushing Fountains Bottled Water."

The huge video screen that was mounted overhead quickly flicked to black. The score of the game was suddenly replaced by nothing, and then by a huge image of a flowing fountain of water. The wet rustling and gurgling of the water as it ran its way down the side of the mountain filled the arena.

Kel couldn't take it anymore. He was going to explode. He let out a loud, inhuman shriek, threw the ball up into the air, and sprinted faster than a man had ever sprinted for the nearest bathroom.

Roger stepped out on the court underneath the basket. An attendant rushed up to him. "I'm sorry, sir, I'll need to see your ticket."

Roger searched his pocket, desperately pawing around for his ticket. Then he remembered, the kid took it. He turned to the attendant to tell him the story. To let him know why he should get another chance. But before a single word escaped his lips, Kel's basketball fell out of the sky on a direct collision course with Roger's head.

Roger looked up as the ball flew towards him. His eyes widened as he had just enough time to realize what was going to happen to him before . . . BAAAAAMMMMM!

CLOSE

"**T**hank you! Thank you very much! You are too kind. Welp, you made it to the end of another fun-filled adventure."

"Yeah! And this time everything worked out exactly like we planned."

"Kel, what are you talking about? Nothing worked out at all like we had planned."

"Really? I thought your plan was to lose the five thousand dollars, get busted by your parents for sneaking out of the house, get cornered by the McThunks and forced to pay them for all the orange soda I drank, and to knock your dad unconscious with a basketball."

"Nah, Kel, I didn't plan on any of those things to happen."

"It's too bad, Kenan, because if you had that would have been one sucessful plan. Op! Wooooooooo!"

"Kel, why are making all those noises?"

"I just realized something."

"What?"

"I still haven't gone to the bathroom yet. Eeeepp! Ackackakca!"

"Well why don't you go then?"

"Okay."

"No wait, Kel, I didn't mean right here."

"But you said—"

"Never mind what I said."

"Well, Kenan, where should I go then?"

"You should grab an honest lawyer, a doughnut hole, and the Loch Ness Monster and meet me at the Ferris wheel. Now come on, wheelie!"

"Kenan? Do they have a bathroom at the Ferris wheel? Kenan? How am I supposed to grab any of those things, none of them really exist! Kenan, why must you always drag me into these things? Kenan? Kenan? Awwwww, here it goes!"

About the Author

STEVE HOLLAND currently resides in Los Angeles with his wife, Hannah. He has written for several Nickelodeon shows, including *Kenan & Kel* and *All That*. He is also the author of *All That: Fresh Out of the Box* and *Good Burger 2 Go*.